KISSES

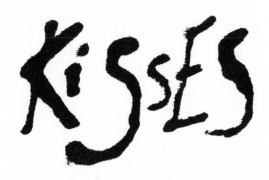

JUDITH CASELEY

Alfred A. Knopf • New York

This is a Borzoi Book
Published by Alfred A. Knopf, Inc.

Copyright © 1990 by Judith Caseley
Jacket art copyright © 1990 by Royce Becker
All rights reserved under International and Pan-American
Copyright Conventions. Published in the United States by
Alfred A. Knopf, Inc., New York, and simultaneously in
Canada by Random House of Canada Limited, Toronto.
Distributed by Random House, Inc., New York.

Manufactured in the United States of America
10 9 8 7 6 5 4 3 2 1

Library of Congress Cataloging-in-Publication Data
Caseley, Judith. Kisses / Judith Caseley. p. cm.
Summary: Eleventh-grader Hannah, talented in music but
lacking in self-confidence, comes to realize, after several un-
successful encounters with boys, the importance of being
true to oneself and of looking beyond outward appearance.
ISBN 0-679-80166-9   ISBN 0-679-90166-3 (lib bdg.)
[1. Self-confidence—Fiction.   2. Intepersonal relations—
Fiction.   3. Music—Fiction.   4. Family   life—Fiction.
5. Friendship—Fiction] I. Title. PZ7.C2677K1 1990
[Fic]—dc20   89-15221

For my father

KISSES

1

The bus screeched to a stop and the doors opened. An old man, wheezing as he pulled himself up the steps, settled with a long sigh into the seat next to Hannah. A sour smell wafted toward her. Hannah pulled her new jean jacket as close to her as possible and tried to open a window. She couldn't. Embarrassed, she looked around to see if anyone had noticed. The woman on the other side of the old man pulled a handkerchief out of her purse and held it to her nose.

The old man leaned toward Hannah. Please don't talk to me, she thought, but she could feel his breath on her face as he wheezed, "Got any money?" Hannah shook her head. She fumbled with the top metal button on her jacket and tried to force it through the stiff opening of the denim. The man wheezed again. Hannah opened her purse and felt around for a stick of gum, a Life Saver, anything. Alarmed, she snapped her purse shut. He might think she was looking for money. Would she call too much attention to herself if she moved? Hannah craned her neck and saw a single vacant seat at the back of the bus.

She rose and made her way to the end of the aisle.

Squeezing past a young man and woman, Hannah sank into the seat. She pulled at the window lever, and the window opened. Gratefully she stuck her nose out the window, like a dog enjoying a car ride.

Hannah heard a licking sound. Was someone eating an ice cream cone? She looked around and felt her face get hot. Next to her the young man was licking the woman's ear. His hand traveled down her side and slid under her sweater. Hannah couldn't see the woman's face, only her red nails against the man's blond hair.

A flashing Dairy Barn sign signaled Hannah's stop, and she rang the bell. She squeezed past the nuzzling couple to the rear exit and pushed open the doors into the street.

Hannah breathed deeply. She opened her purse and took out her mirror, which was shaped like a pair of bright pink lips. She peered at her face. Her father always told her it was a beautiful face, a cross between Ingrid Bergman and Grace Kelly. "Grace Kelly was a blonde," she told him, but he just laughed and said it didn't matter, the beauty went deeper. "A nose like your grandfather's," her grandmother said, and that was why the ladies at Grandma's swim club thought she was a *shiksa*. None of it mattered, really. No one was kissing Hannah on a bus, that much was certain.

Hannah looked around furtively and held the mirror farther away from her. She tried to survey her hips. Definitely too big. Pear-shaped, and nowhere near Grace Kelly's hourglass figure. Her father was crazy. A letter carrier wheeled his bag past Hannah and looked at her curiously. She threw the mirror into her purse and started for home.

Hannah's mother had the same hips. Hannah noticed them the minute she entered the kitchen. They moved with a steady rhythm as her mother diced onion on her wooden chopping board. Hannah watched critically. Sometimes the rear end of her history teacher, Ms. Ferraro, jiggled as she wrote on the blackboard. Hannah noted with relief that her mother's didn't jiggle. She was dressed like Hannah's image of a math teacher, a brown suit and matching low-heeled shoes, a cream-colored blouse, no makeup. Hannah secretly wished her mother would wear some makeup, a little lipstick, a touch of mascara. Mary Plunkett's mother looked like a model and so did Mary. Hannah's hair was straight and long, chestnut brown like her mother's, but her mother wore it short and neat, almost geometric. But she would, wouldn't she, being a math teacher.

Hannah felt guilty and pushed away thoughts of her mother's plainness. She would probably look just like her in twenty years' time. Her mother turned, her eyes crinkling in the corners as she smiled.

"How was school?" She was pulling apart pieces of broccoli now and handed a green floret to Hannah.

Hannah popped it into her mouth and made a face. "Needs some onion dip," she said.

"Too fattening," said her mother, and she leaned past Hannah for the salt shaker. Small-chested, no cleavage. Hannah groaned and sank noisily into a chair at the kitchen table.

"What's the matter?"

"It's fitness month at school. Mrs. Cohn is combining the girls' gym class with the boys'." Hannah rested her cheek on the cool surface of the table. "I'll never survive it."

"Sounds like fun," said her mother.

"Sounds like torture. I'm staying home sick. I need

Richard Milliken looking at me in my gym shorts? Watch." Hannah sprang up and did two jumping jacks. "My fat bounces up and down."

Her mother laughed. "You're not fat, and who's Richard Milliken?"

"He's only the cutest guy in the eleventh grade," said Hannah. "And he doesn't know I exist."

"He'll find out in gym, won't he?" Her mother looked at her slyly. "All that fat bouncing up and down will catch his attention."

"Very funny. I just lost my appetite."

"Spaghetti and meatballs for supper." Her mother sang out the word *meatballs*. Almost a taunt. "Why don't you practice your violin while I finish up? Don't you have an audition this Saturday?"

Hannah didn't want to practice. She wanted to go upstairs, shut the bathroom door, and put cotton between her toes, like Deirdre, and paint her toenails with Crimson Crush. And on her full lips, French Nude. She had bought it because it sounded like sex. She yearned for some red nail polish, like the woman on the bus. She would gladly run her fingers through Richard Milliken's hair, on the back of a bus, on the moon, anywhere. But you can't play the violin with long gleaming-red fingernails. Mr. Kreutzer would have a heart attack on the spot.

She sulked instead. "I hate practicing."

"You're very privileged to be talented," her mother said primly.

"Lucky me. The only one at school trying out for all-state orchestra. The school nerd." Hannah dragged her feet to the closet and opened it. She removed a sleek black case and laid it on the couch. She flipped open the latches, and the familiar smell of rosin filled her nostrils.

Hannah played a little jig, the kind she imagined were played at square dances in the pioneer days. It always made her mother laugh. Today she came dancing into the living room waving a dishcloth and chanting "Promenade left." Hannah settled comfortably into the music. The anger subsided. She didn't feel like a nerd playing, even when her sister Jean told her that she had a double chin when she played. Heartening news. Thank goodness Richard Milliken never saw her play. "Do your scales," called her mother, returning to the kitchen. Hannah started practicing in earnest.

2

*O*n the morning of the audition it was raining hard. Hannah was awake in bed when she heard the alarm go off in her parents' bedroom. She felt a flutter in her stomach and made no attempt to get up. She heard a thump and muted muttering. The lid of the laundry hamper flapping shut. Padding footsteps. There was a soft knock on her door.

"It's time," said her father. "I'll make us some breakfast."

Her father always made breakfast on weekends. But on test mornings and audition days Hannah couldn't eat a thing. She got up and washed her face, then went downstairs to the kitchen.

"No slippers?" said her father. "Your feet will get cold." He set a plate of steaming scrambled eggs in front of her and went into the garage.

He came back with a pair of his ice-skating socks. "A bit musty, but they'll do," he said, handing them to her.

Hannah put them on and ate a mouthful of egg. Her father drank his coffee. They sat quietly without talking. The Bach piece she planned to play spun around in her head, and she resisted the temptation to practice it once more, pajama-clad, right there in the kitchen.

Her father's voice startled her. "You'll do fine."

"I'm as ready as I'll ever be," she said. She went upstairs and put on the pair of new black corduroys, soft gray shirt, and black boots she had laid out the night before. She kept on her father's socks.

Carefully she took her violin out of the closet and wrapped her raincoat around it. Then, with her music under her arm, she ran to the car. Her father leaned across the seat and unlocked the door for her. He took the case from Hannah and settled it in the back. "Is that okay?"

"Fine," she said tersely. She took a deep breath. Nervous already, and they hadn't even pulled out of the driveway.

Her father turned on the ignition, and Hannah jumped as the radio burst into music. "Sorry," he said, and switched it off quickly. He drove carefully on the wet streets. The windshield wipers flapped in their metronome-like rhythm. Oh, lord, shut the wipers off; she knew she played her scales badly. Now the judges loomed, those impassive, expressionless faces, the whispering behind cupped hands. Her heartbeat quickened.

As they pulled up to the school her father squeezed her hand. "Good luck," he said. "Just call me when you're finished."

Hannah was early. The halls were empty and bright with artificial light. She stood in the entranceway, listening. The only sound was the buzz of fluorescent lighting.

She saw the posted sign with relief. At least she was at the right school on the right day. In the corner stood a wooden easel with a large poster resting on its ledge. It read: TRUMPETS AND TROMBONES, ROOM 506, CLARINETS, ROOM 312, FLUTES, ROOM 311, VIOLINS, ROOM 213. She headed toward the room, cursing the unlucky thirteen. She needed all the help she could get. Positioning herself in the middle of the hall, she sat down on a folding chair. It would never do to be first. Soon she heard the discordant strains of other instruments warming up. A boy appeared and settled directly next to room 213. Unlocking his case, he pressed his violin under his chin and started to play. No hesitation, no show of fear. Brilliant. Hannah opened her case slowly. Don't listen, she told herself. She tuned and retuned, praying for more violinists to arrive. With more noise, maybe she could summon up the courage to practice.

At the end of the hall a tall boy played a large double bass with long, deep strokes of his bow. He played well, but it didn't matter. They wouldn't be competing. Hannah's mouth felt dry, and she moved in his direction toward the water fountain. He was bobbing his head, a jazz musician now, and he gave the bass fiddle a twirl. He continued tapping and plucking, and as she bent over the water fountain she heard a muttered "hunh!" and the music stopped. She let the cool water wash into her mouth. Then she turned and bumped right into him.

The boy laughed. "Nervous?" he asked.

"A little," Hannah lied. "Are you?"

"Not a chance. I'll get first or second chair, if the judges know their stuff." He pushed back his dark brown hair and pointed to Hannah's violin. "More competition with that," he said. "You should have chosen an instrument nobody played. You win prizes that way."

"Maybe I should have," said Hannah. "I guess I'd better practice." She hurried back to her chair. Had she chased him away? She couldn't worry about that now, but on an impulse she called back to him, "Good luck!" He turned and said, "Thanks!" over his shoulder, then added, "I won't need it."

The hall reverberated with sound now as arriving musicians tuned their instruments and started to play. They strained to hear their own music, all technique abandoned as they played louder and louder. Hannah tried not to listen to the other violinists. She felt a tightening in her throat. She closed her eyes, wiped her hands on her sweater. She heard the familiar strains of Bach, her own Bach piece, being played. Her music, the music she had practiced for thirty weeks, two hundred hours, seven days a week, again and again. So beautiful, so eloquent. So much better than Hannah. She looked down at her music, smudged and flipping up at the edges. She wanted to tear it up.

Hannah vowed she wouldn't look. She wouldn't. She played her scales with feeling. A gray-haired woman started calling out names and assigning numbers. She was number forty-two. An even number, not too bad. Her Bach piece was being played again, relentlessly. The playing stopped and a voice sang out, "Thank you so much." Hannah looked, she couldn't help it. A girl with flowing red hair resumed playing, with great flourishes and half-closed eyes. Like a concert violinist, like Heifetz, like the movies. The girl's number, abandoned on the seat beside her, was forty-three.

An hour passed. Hannah practiced a little. She tuned and retuned and rosined her bow until it was thickly covered. Finally she sat and waited as the auditions started and the numbers were called.

"Forty-two," called a woman, and Hannah's heart skipped a beat. She rose. Her bow clattered to the floor, making a small cloud of rosin dust. She picked it up hastily and entered the room.

It was an ordinary classroom. THE WARSAW PACT was scrawled across the blackboard. Three men and two women sat behind a metal table, pencils in their hands. The Warsaw Pact? she thought frantically. Why hadn't they erased it? She was going to her execution. The gray-haired woman she had seen earlier asked her to play some scales.

Hannah's hand trembled. Her heart was beating so loudly she could barely hear the woman's instructions. "Your solo piece," repeated the woman, putting on glasses to read the title. Hannah took a deep breath. Her pulse slowed slightly and she played, pressing hard into the chin rest to keep from shaking. The sight-reading was better, and one judge, an old gentleman, rose and said, "Thank you. Very nice." She was finished. She was alive.

As Hannah left the room the red-haired girl pushed past her on the way in. Let them compare her. She didn't care.

"Hey!" called a voice. "How'd you do?" The boy with the bass fiddle walked toward her.

"Okay," said Hannah. "I'm relieved it's over."

"See you at rehearsal then," he said. "I'm gone."

"I hope so," Hannah called after him, and she took out a quarter and went to phone her father.

3

*H*annah entered the auditorium, her acceptance letter in hand. It had arrived in the mail just a few weeks ago. Eighteenth chair out of forty-five. With her parents, she was jubilant. Deirdre congratulated her. "Maybe you'll meet some guys," she said. "You look cute when you play. Kind of intense." She didn't want to look intense. She wanted to look beautiful, sweepingly beautiful.

She looked around. There were a few familiar faces from the audition. The bass player was talking to a tall girl with a ponytail. They both cradled their stringed instruments, the boy plucking a little tune as the girl talked. He looked around idly and waved to Hannah as she caught his eye.

Hannah brightened and stepped up onto the stage to find her seat. Maybe he wasn't so stuck-up after all. She recognized the face of the boy who had played so brilliantly by the audition door. Second chair. It figured. She took her numbered seat, farther back. All around her, violinists were tuning up and sight-reading the music already on their stands. She leafed through the pages: Prokofiev, great; Mozart—Mr. Kreutzer would be pleased.

The Beethoven looked a little hard. She sighed. The music stand tipped slightly and someone sank into the seat next to her. Hannah couldn't believe it. The red-haired girl! She had done better than the red-haired girl. One chair better than Heifetz.

"This place was a bitch to find." The girl wiped her violin with a chamois cloth.

"I know," agreed Hannah. Her father had found it easily. "My name's Hannah. I saw you at the audition."

"Tonia Carro," said the girl, vigorously rubbing rosin on her bow. "They screwed up."

A bearded man stepped onto the podium and tapped his baton.

"Let me introduce myself," he said in an accent like a Russian count. "I'm Anatole Bloch, and I'll be leading the orchestra. You've been chosen the finest young musicians from all over the state." He loosened his tie and cleared his throat. "Some of you have expressed your dissatisfaction with the ranking system. We did the best we could. There will be no changes." He tapped his baton, a few smacks on a naughty child's buttocks. "We are here for one reason—to make music." He stepped briskly off the podium and bent to consult the first chair.

Hannah leaned toward Tonia. "Why do you say they screwed up?" she whispered.

"I know I'm much better than Leo, and he's seated number eight." Tonia shifted in her seat. "Could you give me a little room, please?" Hannah moved over. She told herself she would not feel guilty.

The conductor mounted the podium again and raised his baton. He flicked open a piece of music. "Page one, Beethoven. Now let's see the sweat fly."

She stumbled through the Beethoven. Tonia was slow turning pages. Sulky. And sly. She raised her eyebrow when Hannah had trouble with a passage. The Prokofiev was better. So beautiful, so romantic. They soared through most of it. Tonia seemed to soften, and Hannah had to forgive her. The music made her too happy to be angry.

After the rehearsal, Hannah wiped down her violin and wrapped it in a velvet cloth. Her father hadn't arrived yet and she stood in the doorway watching the street. Her back hurt, and she tried rotating her shoulders to ease the pain.

There was a tap on her shoulder, and she turned. "See you made it," said the bass player, and Hannah smiled. Her heart was pounding. She felt giddy.

"Did you make first chair?" she asked.

"Third, the fools. Did you see the bowwow with the ponytail? That's Marcy, number one." He hoisted his double bass. "Need a ride?"

Hannah shook her head. "No, thanks, my father is picking me up. What do you mean, bowwow?"

"She's a dog!" He laughed as he ran down the steps. "Hey," he called, walking backward. "My name's Bill. What do I call you?"

"Hannah!" she called after him. "Hannah Gold."

She stepped outside into the cool air. Her father's car pulled up to the curb and she ran to meet him.

Hannah settled into her seat and rolled down the window.

"Dad," she said, "when you were young, if a girl wasn't too pretty, did you call her a dog?"

Her father checked his side-view mirror and pulled out into traffic. "I was no looker myself," he said. "With a small crop of acne and an Adam's apple the size of a grapefruit, I had no right to pass judgment. How was rehearsal?"

Hannah was silent. She tried to imagine her father with acne. "Did you have lots of hair then?"

"A mop," he said, "and I still felt like a goon."

Hannah touched her father's arm. "When did you feel better? I mean, when did you get handsome?"

Her father smiled. "I don't know," he said, switching on the radio. "I just got comfortable."

They rode the rest of the way home without speaking. A psychiatrist on the radio said, "Tell her. Tell your mother you don't like it when she drops in unannounced. Practice on me." The caller hesitated. "Would you mind, Mother . . ." The doctor interrupted. "Tell her. Don't ask her," he said.

Her father laughed. "Your mother should listen to that." He pulled into the driveway and switched off the headlights.

"Am I, Dad?" asked Hannah, sitting in the darkness.

"Are you what?" he said, puzzled.

"A dog."

Mr. Gold pushed open his door. "No," he said, "and whoever said such a thing is a moron." He climbed the steps looking for his house key. "Gotcha," he said, inserting the key. "An utter moron," said Mr. Gold, and they walked into the house.

4

"Telephone," called Mrs. Gold into the steam-filled bathroom. She pulled aside the shower curtain, and Hannah jumped.

"Don't do that to someone who's seen *Psycho,*" she cried, her arms shielding her chest.

"You didn't hear me," whispered her mother. "It's a boy on the phone."

"Oh, no," said Hannah, grabbing a towel. "I'm not dressed."

"He's on the phone, not at the front door. Hurry up!"

Hannah made a quick inventory. Calling on a Wednesday was respectable, not great. Tuesday would have been better. She put on her bathrobe and wrapped a towel around her head. Then she went out and picked up the receiver.

"Hello?" she said, taking a deep breath.

"Hannah? It's Bill. How's it going?"

Hannah tried not to sound too eager. "Fine," she said, wiping some drops of water off her face. "I'm wet from the shower."

"Sounds nice," said Bill. "I want to ask you something."

Hannah pulled the terry-cloth robe closer to her and held her breath.

"What are you doing this Saturday night?"

She wondered if she was supposed to lie. "Nothing. Why?"

Bill hesitated. "I thought maybe you'd want to double date."

The towel slipped off Hannah's head and dropped to the floor. "I'd love it!" she cried.

"Great," said Bill, surprise in his voice. "You'll like him. Lance, I mean. You two would make a good match, and you'll get to meet Joy."

"Joy?" said Hannah.

"My girlfriend." There was a silence. "I told you about her, didn't I?"

"Sure," Hannah said. "Joy."

They arranged for Lance to pick her up, and Hannah carefully hung up the phone. Then she walked into the bathroom, locked the door, and climbed back into the shower. She turned on the hot water and let it run down her face and hair, tears and water, water and tears.

"The nerve," said Deirdre as they walked into the art room, "asking you out for one of his friends." She lowered her voice. "Let's sit by Steve Talbot. He's with Richard, and you need greener pastures."

"I told him I'd go," said Hannah. "I was too shocked to say no."

"Say no to what?" Steve Talbot looked up from a lump of clay. "Don't tell me you can't say no."

"A blind date," said Deirdre. "Hannah's got a blind date."

Hannah turned her head sharply toward Deirdre and felt her face get hot.

"I've gone on a few of those myself." Richard sat down. "Anyone need some scraping tools? Take out your anger on a hunk of clay." He took his index finger and pierced the gray lump.

"Maybe it won't be too bad," said Deirdre.

Richard took a stick and widened the hole. "Maybe he'll be the man of your dreams," he said.

Bobby Mack looked up from the other side of the worktable. He had fastened two clay horns to the top of his head. "I thought I was the man of your dreams," he said, clasping his hands in front of him.

Steve Talbot laughed. "Check out Mack the Knife," he said. "He's horny."

Bobby scowled and removed the horns. "I'm the devil," he said, "and there's my angel." He pointed to Hannah.

Hannah kneaded a lump of clay quietly. Then she looked up.

"Mack," she said, "just grow up."

5

On the afternoon of the blind date Deirdre perched on Hannah's bed and watched her try on clothes. "The skirt's too short—he'll think you're easy."

"But I want to look experienced."

"Then wear your new tight jeans."

Hannah held them up. "They make my rear end look too big." She tossed them aside.

"Your mother will kill you if you don't wear them. She thought they were too much money anyway."

"My mother's not going on a date, I am. What about this?" Hannah held up a blue-checked jump suit.

"Too baggy. Doesn't show off your figure."

"Then it's perfect. Who says I want to show off my figure?"

"He won't know if you're thin or fat."

"Good. He'll think I don't care. Anyway, I don't need to impress someone with a name like Lance."

"His mother must have been crazy. Don't they lance boils or something?"

"You're disgusting."

"I know." Deirdre picked up a mirror. "Speaking of boils,

I've sprouted a zit. Have you got any concealer?" She took the tube Hannah held out and dabbed a drop of cream on her blemish. "What movie are you seeing? I hope it's not a scary one."

"Why not?" Hannah looked alarmed. "I think it's the one about a woman who's stalked by a killer."

"Bad idea. When you get scared, you'll want to jump into Lance's arms. Or hide your head on his shoulder."

Hannah looked directly into Deirdre's eyes.

"How would you like to go on a blind date tonight?" she said.

"I can't," said Deirdre. "I have a pimple."

By six thirty Hannah was dressed and waiting. She kept her eye on the clock in the living room and tried to read a book. Her father was smoking his pipe, and her mother was watering the plants.

She held a trail of leaves in her hand and sprayed it with water. "I wonder why they call this plant a wandering Jew?"

"You married one and tamed one," said Mr. Gold, refilling his pipe with tobacco. "Its Latin name is *Zebrina.*"

Hannah looked up from her book. "It beats the name Lance." She sniffed as her father lit his pipe. "You'll ruin your lungs," she added.

Her mother laughed. "She's been grouching around for a week. But she's right about the smoking!" Her voice got louder and more dramatic. "Our little girl has a date, and you'd think she was going to a funeral!"

"A blind date doesn't count."

"Maybe he'll be nice. Don't be such a pessimist."

The doorbell rang and Hannah stiffened on the sofa. Pulling at her jump suit and crossing and uncrossing her legs, she listened as her mother introduced herself. She tried to look casual. Her father glanced at her and looked away quickly.

"Hannah, Lance is here," her mother called from the hallway.

Hannah sprang up and ran to the foyer. Lance stood, his hands in his pockets, little round wire-rimmed John Lennon glasses perched on his nose. He extended his hand and said, "How are you?" His face reddened and his eyes watered. He sniffled and gasped and sprayed Hannah with an enormous sneeze. Hannah wiped her face with the sleeve of her jump suit. She was not encouraged. She looked at her mother, whose face was apologetic. "Have a wonderful time," her mother said brightly.

Outside, Bill and Joy were huddled in the back seat of Lance's car.

"Let's get a move on. It's cold out here." Bill put his hand on Joy's knee. "Joy, meet Hannah."

Hannah sat in front as far from Lance as possible. She concentrated on the scenery, as if Pizza Hut and Burger King were the most fascinating pieces of architecture she had ever seen. Lance was driving with one hand and blowing his nose with the other. At the red light he fished in his pocket for his nasal spray, then squeezed some into his left nostril. At the stop sign he tended to his right one.

"That's better," said Lance. "How long have you been playing the violin?"

"Oh, since I was seven or eight. First I tried the flute, because I wanted to be in the marching band. But I couldn't get a sound out of it."

Joy spoke up. "After Billy's bass, I like the guitar. It's so mellow."

"The violin's harder," Hannah said quickly. "No frets to tell you where to put your fingers. You need an excellent ear."

Lance smiled and hooked a thumb at her. "She's modest, isn't she?"

"That's unfair," protested Hannah. "Do you want me to make believe I'm not good at the violin?"

"Sensitive, too," said Lance. He reached over toward Hannah and for one second she thought he was making a dive for her. Then he opened up the glove compartment and fished out a Chap Stick. "No, I'm only saying that the violin isn't what you'd call cool. Not like the guitar or the piano, even. Have you heard Billy play jazz? He's hot! Let's face it, if you're camping or at a club or a party, you can't pull out a violin and serenade someone."

Lance was beginning to remind Hannah of someone . . . Bill. That's why Bill liked him. Lance was his clone. Stuck-up. Arrogant. Unhygienic, too. She wasn't sure if God existed. If He or She did, she was being punished.

"Hey! No sulking, Hannah." Bill pushed the back of Hannah's seat with his boot. "He's only teasing, aren't you, Lance?"

"Sure. Lighten up," said Lance.

They pulled up to the movie theater. *A Stranger Screams* was playing. Hannah gazed at the poster by the box office window and felt like laughing out loud. A woman with a look of pure horror on her face had her fist jammed into her mouth. A menacing stranger stood behind her. Before this evening is over, thought Hannah, that might be me.

Bill and Lance bought the tickets while the girls waited. Joy swung her head down to her knees and fluffed her fingers through her hair. Hannah resisted looking at herself in the reflection of the large plate-glass window. She knew that the back of her jump suit was badly wrinkled from sitting in the car. The seat belt had left its mark too. She cast a sidelong glance at Joy. Unwrinkled, despite Bill's hands and arms all over her. There was no justice.

Lance handed Hannah her ticket. "I'd like to pay," she said.

"Next time," he said, taking her hand. His palms were moist and clammy, and it was all Hannah could do to stop herself from pulling away.

Bill led the way, sweeping down the aisle toward the front. The other three followed obediently. They took seats in the second row. "Nice and secluded, huh?" said Bill.

Hannah kept her eyes glued to the screen while Lance hummed tunelessly. Bright red and blue lights darted over the white screen, and Hannah began to get a headache. Bill and Joy whispered in the dark, and Joy giggled, pushing Bill away and then snuggling against him. The credits appeared.

A screaming figure with a knife flashed onto the screen and Hannah gasped. An arm immediately circled her and stayed there. It lay heavily across her shoulders. Hannah tried to shift away, but the arm remained. Her neck began to hurt, and she said a prayer: Let this evening end. Let this movie end. Let me out of here. Halfway through the picture she got up the nerve to slip out from under the arm and go to the ladies' room. She sank gratefully onto the plastic-covered couch. A woman was fixing her lipstick, turning right, then left, then right again, pulling at her dress and flicking at her hair. She was examining her face now, applying more blush. She must like her boyfriend, thought Hannah, to take such pains. The woman sprayed some perfume behind her ears and knees, then turned to see Hannah watching.

"Want some?" she asked. "It's Elizabeth Taylor's Passion."

"No, thanks," said Hannah, feeling nauseous. She didn't need passion. She didn't want passion. She wanted ice cream at home, alone, and a good book. Or tea with her mother. Or popcorn with her father, watching a western. And if Jean wasn't away at school, Scrabble and pretzels and Hannah would win.

She slipped back into the darkened theater and found her seat. The arm found its way across her shoulders and rested there like a lazy boa constrictor. Hannah sighed. She could feel the sweat from Lance's armpit damp on her shoulder. She hoped with all her heart that no one would be hungry after the movie.

"Anyone for ice cream?" Joy looked around eagerly.

Hannah didn't have the heart to say no. Lance and Bill already thought she was a bad sport. "Sure," said Hannah, "all that blood and gore gave me an appetite."

Hannah followed Lance into the Hillside Diner, past the dusty rows of bright plastic flowers, to a booth. Hannah scanned the menu and ordered chocolate ice cream with hot fudge. She remembered hearing that chocolate was an antidepressant . . . it released some chemical in the brain. One spoonful made her feel better.

"Do you play an instrument, Lance?" Hannah asked brightly.

Lance smirked. "Not one that you'd know about. But I hold my own."

"And such stiff competition!" Bill laughed. "You have to work like a dog." The boys laughed uproariously.

Hannah's face reddened. Joy was noisily sucking the last of her soda through her straw. She looked up and said casually, "You guys are gross."

Bill's eyes widened. "Hey, we're talking music here! It's survival of the fittest. You have to keep your nerve up, with the auditions and practicing." He winked at Lance.

"Survival of the fittest." Hannah shook her head. "When I was in biology class, I kept hearing about that. So on one of the exams I wrote about natural selection, and I spelled *fittest* 'phytist'—I thought it was some kind of amoeba or something." She tried to keep the desperation out of her voice. At least she was holding a conversation.

Suddenly Hannah heard a familiar voice in the booth behind them.

"Oh, Pam's all right," said the voice. "I took her out a few times."

"How was it?" asked another voice.

"Let's put it this way. One breast was so big I had to hold it with both hands."

Hannah felt her cheeks burn. It sounded like Richard Milliken talking to Steve Talbot. Please, no. Please leave before we do, she thought. Joy was talking now, and Lance had monopolized Hannah's shoulder again. When they got up to leave, Hannah glanced behind her. The booth was empty.

Outside, Joy and Hannah climbed into the car. Lance whispered hurriedly to Bill, "Echo Lake Park," and Hannah felt a surge of panic. They pulled into a tree-lined street and drove until they reached the park entrance sign. Next to it hung another sign: NO DRINKING, NO LOITERING AFTER DARK. Lance sped into the park and turned the car sharply into a space between two darkened cars. He switched off the ignition. "Lights," he said, swatting the high beams to low. "Camera!" he said, snapping an imaginary picture of Hannah.

"Action!" called Bill from the back seat.

"We used to come here on picnics . . ." Hannah's voice trailed off. They were facing the lake, shimmering in the moonlight. Or was it the low beams of the parked cars reflected on the water? She saw only slight movement in the car next to her, then heard a laugh and a can being tossed out a window. And then the rubbing of cloth on vinyl as Joy and Bill shifted positions in the back seat.

Lance reached over and pulled her close to him. Say no, say no, say no, popped into her head, but she let him kiss her, a lingering kiss. She felt no flickerings of desire. No kindling of passion. She was reminded of an eel with sucking lips, a photograph in her biology book that she tried to avoid when she was leafing through it. She felt absolute and utter disgust.

Lance fumbled with the snaps on Hannah's jump suit and popped three of them open. Hannah took his hands and pushed firmly. "No," she said loudly.

"Come on," said Lance.

"No," said Hannah. "Take me home." She felt better. She was surprised at how easy it was to say. Lance turned on the ignition and gunned the engine. There was a shout from the back seat as Lance reversed the car with a great lurch, and Hannah caught a glimpse of Joy buttoning up her blouse. Lance roared off up the street.

They pulled up to Hannah's house. Lance left the motor

running and leaned across her lap, grunting as he opened the door. Hannah slipped out of the car and heard a vague "See you at rehearsal." She unlocked the front door and crept into the house, shedding her clothes the minute she got to her room. She sniffed the shoulder of her jump suit and felt sick. It smelled of Lance. She rolled it into a ball and stuffed it into the back of her closet. Then she turned off the light and got into bed, lying there with her eyes open. Her last thought before she fell asleep was what she would tell Deirdre. Chocolate helped a little. She might have caught a terrible cold. And on a blind date, never wear clothes that open easily.

6

*I*n English class Hannah took her usual seat in front of Bobby Mack.

He tapped her shoulder and she turned around.

"How strong are you?" he asked.

"Strong enough," she said.

Bobby touched her arm. "Let's see. Hold up two fingers," he said, and Hannah did.

"Now resist, and I'll try to move them with one finger." Hannah held her fingers rigidly in front of her face, and Bobby pulled them. With a snap she hit herself hard in the mouth. She tasted blood and touched her fingers to her lips.

"I'm bleeding," she said. "I've cut my lip and I'm bleeding." She looked accusingly at Bobby and held up a bloody finger.

Bobby's face was ashen. "I didn't think you'd fall for it," he said lamely. "I'm sorry."

Mr. Mandel, the English teacher, walked into the classroom. Picking up an eraser, he rubbed vigorously at the blackboard. PUBLIC SPEAKING, he wrote on the board. He pushed his glasses up his nose and jabbed the air with his finger.

"In my class," he said, "you'll learn to speak, and you'll learn to speak well!" There were groans in the room.

"At least once in a lifetime," continued Mr. Mandel, "you'll need to speak in public—be it at a meeting or a school or even at a wedding. So you may as well start here." He handed out work sheets and said, "On Monday, two weeks from today, be ready with a ten-minute speech on a familiar subject. You'll speak more eloquently about something you know about. Props are allowed, and demonstrations are acceptable. Kite-flying, baton-twirling, bee-keeping, whatever. Just be comfortable with your subject matter."

More work, thought Hannah. Orchestra rehearsal, practicing, a bloody mouth. And now this.

She met Deirdre at the door and they headed for the cafeteria. Hannah stood behind Deirdre in line and lifted a strand of Deirdre's hair. "You look blond," she said. "When did you get so blond?"

Deirdre laughed. "I bleached it," she said. "What do you think of it?"

"It looks . . . different," said Hannah. "I can't get used to it."

"Well, the boys like it. At least Pete Leone does."

"He would," said Hannah sarcastically.

"Hey," said Deirdre, a hurt look on her face. "Are you mad at me for bleaching my hair? Is it that bad? It was only a rinse—it will wash out."

Hannah shook her head. "I'm just jealous, I guess." She leaned forward and tipped her head against Deirdre's shoulder. "Pete will ask you out on a date, and I'll be alone forever, and Richard Milliken likes Pam Porter, or at least he likes her breasts." She lifted her head. "And I don't have any."

Deirdre laughed. "Neither do I!"

"But you're a blonde now. And that's what they like. Big breasts and blond hair. Not brains and a bloody lip."

"You need food. Your brain needs some food." Deirdre craned her head toward the front of the line. "What's keeping them? My friend needs food. She's losing her mind."

"Maybe I should bleach my hair. I need to do something. I feel like such a washout."

"Was it your fault Lance was a jerk? Could I get into all-state orchestra? Come on," said Deirdre as they moved toward the shelves of food. "I'll buy you an ice cream."

They picked up tuna salad sandwiches and cartons of orange juice, and Deirdre paid for two ice creams. They made their way to an empty table.

"Your hair looks nice," said Hannah, ripping the plastic wrap off her sandwich. "You look . . . perky. I need to do something drastic. Nobody looks at me. Men don't even whistle at me in the street. Maybe I should streak my hair purple."

"No way," said Deirdre. "It's not you. Just be yourself. You're . . . stately."

Hannah snorted. "You sound like my father. Stately! A mansion is stately." She tossed aside the remains of the sandwich and tore the wrapper off her ice cream. "And how can I be myself when I don't know who I am? I only know what I want to be. Like you—witty and pretty."

"Perky and jerky. Give me a break," said Deirdre. "The

boys are just lined up and knocking down the door. You're tall, you're gorgeous, you're talented. So you're flat-chested. They won't hang down when you're an old lady."

"What won't hang down when you're an old lady?" A tray landed with a thump on their table. "Is this seat taken?" asked Bobby Mack. Without waiting for an answer, he spread out his juice, French fries, grilled cheese sandwich, and chocolate cake. "I need to take nourishment."

"Take nourishment?" said Deirdre. "Pig out!"

Bobby laughed. "Funny," he said. "How come your friend isn't laughing?"

"Because you're a menace," said Hannah.

"Don't be so hard on him." Deirdre patted Bobby's cheek. "He's close to tears as it is, aren't you, Bobby?"

Bobby made a mournful face and scratched his head. "She doesn't love me, and I don't know what to do," he sniffled, wiping imaginary tears from his eyes.

Hannah crumpled her napkin into a ball and threw it. It bounced off Bobby's forehead, dropping neatly onto his chocolate cake. "I have an idea," she said.

"What?" said Deirdre and Bobby in unison.

"Maybe," said Hannah, "you should do your speech on how to be a pain in the butt." She gathered together her books and purse and stood up. "It's what you're good at. Coming, Deirdre?" she said, and walked out the door.

7

Gym class was first period, and Hannah hated it. She wasn't one of the miserable few girls left behind when teams were chosen. It wasn't that. She was always somewhere in the middle. Never one of the chosen few, the athletes with their strong, sleek thighs who always seemed to be doing runners' stretches. She played music the way they ran. That was her runner's high—her heart opened up and her pulse quickened in a crescendo of sound and feeling. There was nothing like it. But she envied the girls who came in first on the mile run, mouths parted, sweat glistening, firm legs pumping, and the click of the stopwatch recording their triumph. She longed to be one of them, with their simple golden talent.

In the locker room Hannah struggled into her blue gym shorts and white shirt. She looked down at her chest as if perhaps today two rounder bumps would surface. But no, she was still the same, flat-chested and much too tall. Last summer, when her uncle came to dinner and had too much wine, he told Jean that she had breasts like melons, and Hannah's were like strawberries. After that, she'd lost her taste for strawberries.

Hannah walked into the gymnasium cautiously. The boys were nowhere in sight, but there was already a different feeling about the gym. She heard sneakers squeaking, not the usual gossiping in corners. Pam and Rebecca played basketball furiously. Pam leaped into the air and hooked the ball into the ring, clapping her hands rapidly and running in place when she made the basket. Hannah couldn't help but notice Pam's breasts bounce under her thin blouse. She looked away quickly.

Mrs. Cohn, the gym teacher, strode briskly to the front of the gym. She bent down and flattened her hands to the floor. She had small, round buttocks, taut hamstrings, runner's thighs. The boys' gym teacher approached her and snapped the waistband of her shorts. She stood quickly, annoyance fading to pleasure as he cupped his hand to her ear and whispered something. Hannah wondered if they were flirting.

Hannah tucked her blouse into her shorts and checked to see that all her buttons were done up. A black-and-blue mark glared on her right thigh. Her shorts would not cover it. The boys were watching. . . . Their eyes were everywhere.

"That's Mr. Arson," Hannah heard Pam say. "He could light a fire under me any day." Hannah could feel herself blush as Rebecca giggled loudly and gave Pam a shove. Mr. Arson was old! At least thirty, anyway. But maybe that wasn't old to Pam. Pam had lots of dates. Pam was experienced.

"Okay, everybody," called Mrs. Cohn. "Let's have lines of ten. We're starting our coed fitness program today, so be on your best behavior. Ten minutes of warm-up calisthenics." Mrs. Cohn's voice echoed in the huge gymnasium. She fluffed out her short hair and started rotating her head from left to right.

Mr. Arson joined her. "I'll lead off with some exercises," he said, "and then I'll pick someone to continue." He smiled at Mrs. Cohn, who flashed him a smile back and rotated her head the other way.

They were flirting for sure. Mrs. Cohn reminded Hannah of Deirdre. Perky. Perky and athletic. She was probably a cheerleader in high school, with lots of boyfriends.

They did fifty stomach crunches. Hannah couldn't keep her hands behind her head on the last ten. She stopped herself from grunting. The push-ups were worse, but most of the girls didn't care. They wanted firm stomachs but they didn't care about their arms. They did them modified style, knees bent. Some of the athletic girls did them regular style, on their toes, rapidly. Hannah was glad when they were over.

"The girl with the long brown hair," said Mr. Arson, pointing to Hannah.

Hannah looked behind her.

"Yes, you," he called. "The tall young lady."

"You, Hannah," called Mrs. Cohn. "Lead us in some more exercises."

Hannah walked slowly to the front. Her heart was pounding, audition-style. But this was the grand slam of auditions—they were scrutinizing the back of her, the front of her, her hips, her buttocks, her wilted blouse, her black-and-blue mark. The lines of alternating boys and girls loomed in front of her. She cleared her throat and pulled down the back of her shorts.

"Donkey kicks, forty times each leg," she said, and she counted aloud as she bent and kicked one leg out and then the other from a squatting position. She willed her thighs to stop shaking, her shorts to stop hiking up. They finished the exercise, and her mind went blank. Quickly, think of another one. "Squat thrusts," she said hastily. "Twenty times." There was a chorus of groans and she realized with horror that she had picked another difficult one. They would hate her. Breathing hard, Hannah tried to think of an easy exercise. She looked in desperation at Mrs. Cohn.

"Jumping jacks," Bobby Mack suggested, so Hannah called out jumping jacks, twenty times. She thanked him silently.

After the calisthenics, the boys were told to head for the boys' gymnasium. "Keep your lines!" called Mr. Arson, and they filed out, expanding their chests as they moved past the girls.

"Bye-bye, Richie," said Pam as Richard Milliken strutted past her.

"Bye-bye, Pammie," said Richard, and he winked at Hannah. "Not bad, Hannah. Some hips."

"Deirdre," said Hannah, "it is not a compliment. It means big hips." She leaned back against the pillows on her bed and propped the phone under her chin. "It means fat."

"If he meant fat, he would have said so. He could have said 'Not bad for a fatso,' right? He said he liked them."

"Sure, and he said it in front of Pam," wailed Hannah, punching a pillow into the corner of the bed. "Pam of the big breasts! She got a good laugh out of it."

"What can I say? I think you're a much nicer size, anyway." Deirdre hesitated. "Pete called me." She paused. "He asked me out."

Hannah was quiet for a moment. Then she took a deep

breath. "That's great!" she said brightly. "When are you going?"

"This Saturday," Deirdre said quickly. "Wish me luck."

"Good luck," said Hannah. "And no jump suits!" They both laughed, and Deirdre said good-bye.

Hannah reached over to the bureau and picked up a large hand mirror. She lay back on the bed and directed the mirror toward her hips. They seemed to spread against the mattress and look larger. She could never lie down with a boy. Maybe he would be so close to her it wouldn't matter.

She got up and brushed her hair with long, punishing strokes, aiming for one hundred. At twenty-five she eased up. At thirty-five she threw down the brush in disgust. "Stupid," she said. She ran her fingers through her hair. It felt soft, luxurious. Wouldn't a boy like it? She heard laughter in the kitchen and she went downstairs. Maybe her mother would cheer her up.

Her parents were sitting at the kitchen table, their half-empty teacups in front of them. Her father was eating the last cookie.

"I've missed tea," Hannah said dejectedly.

"I'll make some more," said her mother, and soon the kettle was whistling cheerfully.

Hannah looked around the bright yellow kitchen. It had been yellow for as long as she could remember. There were framed pictures of ripe fruits and vegetables on the walls, and pots of flowering plants on the counters. Her parents looked so happy. She felt like a stray puzzle piece that didn't fit in anywhere.

Her mother stood at the counter, her back to Hannah, and fixed Hannah's tea. Hannah looked at her father. He must like her mother's figure, her mother's hips. She took the steaming cup of tea from her mother and stirred some sugar into it. Her father ran his hand along his wife's arm.

"Do you like Mom's hips?" Hannah blurted out.

Her father looked surprised. He smiled at her mother. "I told your mother when I met her that I liked her child-bearing hips."

Her mother rolled her eyes. "I was insulted. I told him he was complimenting a large pelvis. Not very romantic."

"So you liked them," persisted Hannah. She swallowed some tea and felt her tongue burn.

"I've always liked them fine," said her father. "You take after your mother. You have her good legs, too."

"Great," said Hannah glumly. He obviously expected her to burst into song. She sipped her tea slowly and listened to them chat about the President's latest misdeeds, potassium in bananas, and checking labels for the dreaded palm oil. Somehow the conversation did not cheer her up. She didn't care that aluminum foil could cause Alzheimer's disease. She had big hips, a bloody lip, a burned tongue, and no date on Saturday night.

She left the bright kitchen and went to practice her violin.

8

*A*ll week Hannah had practiced her orchestra pieces diligently. She entered the auditorium for rehearsal, aware that this time her pulse did not quicken. She felt more confident and was eager to play. She would not let Tonia's sulking upset her. Taking a seat in the back of the darkened hall, she looked guardedly around. She had no urge to see Bill and be humiliated by him. A few seats away a boy was snoring gently. He looked so peaceful, his hand covering his face and a finger moving each time he snored. The sound lulled her. So what if Bill made fun of her? Deirdre was right. Lance was a jerk who thought the price of a movie and a dish of ice cream meant he could explore her favorite jump suit. She had the right to say no! Hannah nodded her head sharply. She looked up and saw two eyes watching her. The sleeping figure was awake.

"You look awfully serious," he said.

"I'm giving myself a lecture," said Hannah.

He raised an eyebrow.

"To have the courage of my convictions," she said. Out of the corner of her eye she could see Bill coming into the auditorium with his arm around Tonia. They came closer, deep in conversation. "Of *course* you play the violin better than she does," she heard Bill say, "but what can you do?" His eyes traveled to Hannah. "Mediocrity triumphs," he said.

Hannah's cheeks burned. She turned to her neighbor.

"My name's Hannah. What instrument do you play?" she asked, concentrating on ignoring Bill.

"Trumpet," he said. "George Goldberg," he added. "You play the violin. I've seen you."

Hannah was flattered. She'd never noticed him before, but there wasn't that much to notice. Nondescript brown hair, a long face, pale skin, pale eyes.

"I've seen you with that guy." He nodded toward Bill. "What's he trying to do, give you your comeuppance?"

Hannah smiled ruefully. "I guess so. I had a blind date with one of his friends, and I didn't like him." She felt grown-up and almost experienced.

"I see," said George. "Revenge. Well, those two are made for each other. She acts like she has a stick up her."

Hannah laughed. "Maybe she does. She's always telling me to move over and give her more room. I'd like to move right off the stage!"

"Don't do that," said George. "I'd miss you." His hand plucked at his collar, straightening a tie that wasn't there.

Was he blushing? Hannah wondered. He'd been watching her. Maybe he had a crush on her like she had on Richard.

She smiled at George. "I like the trumpet," she said. "I tried to play the flute when I was younger, but I couldn't get a sound out of it. I guess I don't have the lips for it."

"You have nice lips," said George, getting up suddenly.

He *is* blushing. Hook, line, and sinker, thought Hannah. Wait until I tell Deirdre.

They walked down the aisle and up the steps to the stage. George Goldberg and Hannah Gold. Grandma Molly would be in seventh heaven. She would personally erect a *huppah* on the stage and drink a toast to the bride and groom.

"See you later," called Hannah, "at break time?" She was brave now, and confident that he would say yes.

George bobbed his head and said, "You can share my fruit and stuff. My mother says talent needs energy." He made a face and added quickly, "Mothers!"

"Great," she said. His mother? Oy! She lifted her violin to her shoulder. Bill was watching, she was sure of it.

George Goldberg called on Monday night. The moment the phone rang, Hannah knew. Her heart didn't hammer, her palms didn't sweat. "Wipe that smug look off your face, you wench," said her father. "The poor boy is smitten."

Hannah didn't run to the phone. She held the receiver casually, as if Deirdre were on the other end.

"Hi, George, what's up?" she said.

"Nothing much," said George.

"Oh," said Hannah. She waited for him to get up his nerve.

"I was wondering." George coughed and cleared his throat.

"Yes?" He sounded as if he were strangling.

"Would you like to go out to dinner this Saturday? I just got my license, and my mother said I could borrow the car." George rushed on. "Maybe you know a restaurant you'd like to go to?"

Hannah didn't hesitate. "The Peking Duck, on Route Twenty-two," she said. Deirdre had gone there with Pete, and it sounded fancy and grown-up.

"Peking Duck it is," said George. "Do we need a reservation?"

"Oh, I don't think so," said Hannah.

"What time should I pick you up?"

"About six thirty." They said good-bye and she hung up the phone. Hannah was going out to dinner with a boy. A boy who was crazy about her.

9

George still hadn't arrived at seven o'clock. Hannah was dressed and ready. Her hair was sleekly held back by a new leopard headband that was giving her a headache.

She wore a soft black lamb's wool sweater, a woolen skirt, and black heels that hurt her feet. She was furious. George was late.

"Ten more minutes and I'm out of these clothes," said Hannah.

"Give him twenty, the roads are bad," said her mother.

"It's a snow flurry, the roads are clear." Hannah twisted her amber beads. "He doesn't respect me if he's late."

"You'll break that necklace and then I won't loan you anything of mine again." Her mother looked nervously at her watch.

The doorbell rang and Hannah sprang off the couch. She yanked open the door.

"Boy, you like to keep a girl waiting," she said.

George stood there in a thick woolen hat with ear flaps.

Beads of sweat dotted his forehead. "I'm so sorry, Hannah," he said. "I got lost."

Hannah softened a little. His mother probably made him wear that goofy hat. "Let's go," she said. "I'm starving." She took his arm and called out to her parents that they were leaving.

Her mother appeared. "Drive safely," she said, extending her hand to George. "It's nice to meet you, George." Her father came in. "And no drinking," he said, patting George on the shoulder. Her mother shushed him a low voice.

"I will," said George, confused. He was perspiring profusely now. "We won't," said Hannah, and she slammed the door behind them.

They got lost again. George drove jerkily and braked often. Hannah felt like she was in a bumper car at an amusement park.

"It's the stick shift," he explained. "I didn't learn on a stick, and it takes some getting used to."

Hannah nodded. She wasn't thrilled by him. There were no tingles running up and down her spine. She roused herself and told him about English class and the speech she had to give.

"But what should I give it on?" she said. "I thought batik, but my best friend Deirdre is doing that. We learned together last summer. I have to spend all day tomorrow writing it."

"How about the violin?" said George. "You could do a demonstration and talk about its history."

"Not bad, George," But could she play in front of the whole class? And confirm herself as a nerd?

44

"Route Twenty-two!" said George. "The Peking Duck!"

"Food!" said Hannah. She would never dare let Richard Milliken know how much she enjoyed her food. With Richard, if it ever happened, she would just nibble. Poor George. With him she could pig out.

Hannah thought the restaurant looked expensive. It had brocade on the walls and a miniature pagoda in the center of the room. Her father would have called it garish. Her mother would have laughed at the pagoda.

A dainty Chinese woman in a flowered silk dress seated them and gave them huge tasseled menus. "What shall we eat?" said Hannah.

George gazed at the menu as if it were a test he had forgotten to study for. He turned the pages and squinted.

"I've never had Chinese food before," he said.

"You're kidding!" Hannah hoped she remembered how to use chopsticks. "Do you want me to order for us?"

"Okay," said George, looking relieved.

The waiter poured them cups of tea, and they munched handfuls of crunchy noodles. "Once, when I went to Chinatown with my grandmother, there was a cigarette butt the color of the noodles. Right on top of the bowl, camouflaged." Hannah examined a golden noodle. "Grandma made us leave." The waiter set the steaming bowls of wonton soup Hannah had ordered in front of them.

George picked at his wonton like a chemistry student dissecting a frog. "What's in it?" he asked, pushing it with a chopstick so that it swam across his bowl.

"It's noodles and scallion and bits of pork." Hannah speared one and ate it with relish.

"I think I'll skip it." George stirred the broth with his chopstick and looked around hungrily.

"It's delicious," said Hannah. "Try the Peking Duck Delight." She ladled a portion onto his plate.

George sniffed at a spoonful and said suspiciously, "What is this?"

"It's either shrimp or scallops," said Hannah.

"Oh." George carefully placed the morsel of seafood back onto his plate. "I see."

Hannah slammed down her chopsticks. They flipped across the table like giant pick-up sticks. "What do you mean, I see? You haven't eaten a single thing, George. What did we come here for if you don't even like Chinese food?" She looked around to see if they were being watched, if people could tell she was dating a nerd.

George clicked his chopsticks together nervously. "I thought the Peking Duck Delight meant chicken. I guess I have a problem."

"What, ulcers?"

"No." He laid the chopsticks carefully on his plate. "My parents keep a kosher home," he said. "I just can't eat this stuff, Hannah."

Hannah sighed. "Why didn't you tell me?"

"I wanted to make you happy," said George simply.

The waiter arrived and looked questioningly at the food. "Is everything okay?" he asked.

"We're finished," said Hannah. She watched as the waiter scraped together a large mound of Peking Duck Delight. He gathered up the dishes deftly, whisked them away, and returned with a dish of cookies.

Hannah poured George some tea. "Eat the almond cookie, George," she said. "You must be starving." She cracked open a fortune cookie for herself and removed the strip of paper.

YOU ARE ABOUT TO EMBARK ON A GREAT ROMANCE. Hannah threw the strip of paper into her teacup. It floated in the amber liquid. Then she ate the cookie. So much for fortunes.

10

Hannah listened, her palms sweaty, as Deirdre demonstrated the art of batik. Her violin lay in its case across her lap. She had no idea if she would get to play today. Deirdre was in her element now: melting paraffin wax on a burner, pulling a piece of cotton sheet across a stretcher and stapling it smooth. Halfway through, as she was dipping her brush in the hot wax, she burned her hand. "Excuse me, kind audience," she said between clenched teeth, and she ran to the bathroom. She came back, her hand wrapped in a wet paper towel, and said, "Did you miss me?" She shot a look at Mr. Mandel. "That's not part of the speech," she said. She finished by dripping wax on the piece of sheet in the shape of a bird. After immersing the cloth in a bowl of blue dye, she lifted it out with a wide smile. Her hands were bright blue. "Rubber gloves would help." Deirdre laughed. Everyone applauded.

Mr. Mandel consulted his list and made a note. Hannah's pulse quickened. It wasn't audition fear. It didn't really matter how well she played. She felt more like she was about to lead the exercises in gym class—stark naked. And if she had burned her hand in front of the whole class, she knew she would have burst into tears—with hiccups, probably.

"Bobby Mack," called Mr. Mandel. Bobby stood up quickly and said, "That's me!" He ran into the hallway. There was a crash and a clatter, and he wheeled in a cart with a strange metal contraption on it.

"The subject of my speech," said Bobby, shuffling index cards, "is something I'm an expert at." He reached into a paper bag.

"Hot dogs," he said. "Kielbasa, to be precise. Polish sausages. My father is Polish, and his mother taught him to make sausages, as her mother taught her. Every Saturday, my father would set up his grinder"— Bobby pointed to the metal contraption—"and he would take his pig's intestine . . . Has everybody had breakfast?" There were loud groans as he held up a thin membranous tissue like something straight out of a horror movie. "Then he took his meat and ground it, adding seasoning." Bobby held out a bowl of chopped meat and peered into it. "Smells a little funny. I couldn't find the ice pack." There were more groans. Bobby widened his eyes. "Hey. I'm at a very delicate part now. We attach the pig's intestine to this spout here . . ." Bobby paused, held out his hands, and directed the crescendo of moaning. "And"—he turned the handle of the machine—"Voilà! Kielbasa. Throw it in the smoke box, and it's."—he kissed his hand with a flourish—"delicious."

Bobby proceeded to give a short history of sausage and explained the various cultures that have a form of it. "Think about it," he said. "We have hot dogs, hot sausage, sweet sausage, bologna, salami, wontons. Did I say wontons? Maybe I'm in the blintze family now. Does anyone know the Chinese form of sausage?" There was scattered laughter, and Bobby held up his index finger. "As a closing remark, I'd like to say: Those of you who think I'm full of bologna . . ." Bobby tied the end of the sausage and dangled it in the air.

"I am." And he dropped the sausage on Hannah's desk with a flourish.

Richard Milliken was walking right toward her. There was no doubt about it. Deirdre called him "the Strut" because he walked a little like John Travolta in *Saturday Night Fever*. For Hannah it was true sex appeal. Her heart fluttered as he gave her locker a few metallic-sounding knocks.

"Anyone home?" he said.

"Only us mice," said Hannah, wondering what on earth she meant. She wished desperately that she could banter like Deirdre.

"So what did you think of the speeches today?" he said.

"Fine," said Hannah, fiddling with her combination. She swung open the locker door and pointed to her violin. "Only I'm still waiting to give mine."

"Too bad. So you have to lug that thing in every day?"

"Yup," said Hannah. "I'm developing my biceps." She flexed her muscles like a body-builder. Would he think she was funny?

He laughed. "It's a good thing you don't play the tuba."

"Can you just see me?" She filled her cheeks with air, expanding them like balloons, then stopped herself from demonstrating an imaginary tuba. Don't push it. Stop auditioning. She spoke to herself sternly.

Richard gave her lock a twirl. "So what's going on between you and the Mack truck?"

"Nothing at all," said Hannah indignantly. "Mutual dislike."

He knocked on the locker again. "He's giving you presents, Hannah."

"Like what?" said Hannah, amazed.

"Knockwurst," said Richard. "In Mandel's class."

"Very funny. Actually, it's kielbasa," she corrected him. "And what about you? I hear it takes two hands to hold one of Pam's breasts." Oh, God, she'd said it. Please let him be deaf in both ears.

"What a mouth," said Richard, his face pale. "And you look like such a nice girl." He stood still for a moment, then gave the locker a final knock. "Later," he said, and walked off.

"Stupid, stupid, stupid," Hannah said. She shook her head. Talking to yourself out loud was a sign of madness. Maybe she was going crazy. She pressed her forehead against the locker door.

"Are you all right?" said a voice. Mrs. Cohn looked at Hannah curiously.

"No!" said Hannah violently. She turned and saw Mrs. Cohn's sympathetic face. "I mean, yes. I'm okay." She made a vow. She wouldn't talk about her problems. Not to perky Mrs. Cohn.

Mrs. Cohn walked past her and stopped. "How about walking me to my car?" she said.

They left the school and the cold air hit them. Hannah buttoned up her coat and wrapped her scarf around her neck.

"You can tell me to mind my own business," said Mrs. Cohn, tucking her hair into a beret, "but I'm a good listener."

Hannah hesitated. She broke her vow of silence in an instant. "I'm an idiot," she said. "I just made a total fool of myself."

"It happens," said Mrs. Cohn, taking Hannah's arm and skirting a patch of slushy snow.

"I just can't talk to them," said Hannah. "Boys. I don't know how."

Mrs. Cohn laughed. "I think they feel the same about us," she said.

They passed the schoolyard. Some boys were throwing a football around, jacketless.

"They must be freezing!" said Hannah.

Mrs. Cohn smiled. "Or crazy," she said.

A football thudded in front of them, and Hannah heard a breathless "I'll get it." Pam scooped up the ball and tossed it over the metal fence. "Nice pass," called Steve Talbot. "How's your tackle?" Pam laughed, all glistening red lips and white teeth. "Try me," she said.

"She's good with the passes," said Hannah between her teeth.

"Touché," said Mrs. Cohn.

"And she always gets the guys," said Hannah, instantly wishing she hadn't said it. Pam and Steve were talking intently now, shoulders touching.

"So?" Mrs. Cohn turned and looked directly at her. "You're a terrific girl, Hannah. You're sweet, you're attractive. You've just got one problem."

"A big mouth," said Hannah.

"No," said Mrs. Cohn, laughing again. "You sell yourself short." She pulled a set of keys out of her pocket and stopped in front of an old sedan with a dented fender. "Do me a favor," she said, inserting a key in the door. "Ease up on yourself."

Hannah went home and dialed Deirdre's number.

"So what do you think?" she said, finishing her story.

"What do I think?" Deirdre paused. "I think the Strut and the Mouth are a match made in heaven."

Hannah had a boyfriend, there was no doubt about it. But his name was George, not Richard. He called her often and shared cookies with her at rehearsal. She couldn't understand why she wasn't happier. There was a gnawing, a buzz of unhappiness in her head, like some disease of the ear she had read about. Some people went crazy from it—a constant noise, a ringing, a ticking.

So it must have something to do with George. He was a decent fellow, her father said. A nice boy, said her mother. A nice nerd, thought Hannah, or maybe a semi-nerd.

Deirdre was dating Pete, and Hannah had gotten used to seeing them together, Pete's arm slung around Deirdre's neck, cave-man style. Pete was older, and he looked a little dangerous to Hannah. Hooded eyes and a very short military haircut. Secretly she thought he looked like an ex-convict.

"George sounds nice," said Deirdre as they walked to the library. "At least he wants to please you. Pete tells me what we're doing and when we're doing it, no questions asked." Deirdre shook her blond hair that Pete loved so well. "Has he kissed you yet?"

"Yes," said Hannah glumly. "Long wet ones, and that's it. I feel like asking him to brush his teeth. How can you stand it? Doesn't Pete smoke?"

Deirdre thought a minute. "He does smoke," she said, "but it doesn't bother me. I guess I like him too much to care."

"Richard hasn't said a word to me since I opened my big mouth," said Hannah. "And I'll probably make a fool of myself again when I finally give my speech."

"Are you still going to teach someone to play a song?"

"I told you I was. Otherwise they'll be bored to death." Hannah plucked a sprig of holly off a bush. "He loves me, he loves me not . . ."

Deirdre snatched the leaves from Hannah and threw them into the air. "You won't need these!" she said excitedly.

"What are you talking about? Give me back my holly."

Deirdre looked smug. "Pick Richard," she said.

Hannah looked blank.

"For your demonstration! Pick Richard." Deirdre bent and picked up the holly. "You may have these back now. You're up to 'he loves me not.'" She dangled the sprig in front of Hannah.

Hannah didn't take it. A light was dawning, slowly. "Should I really pick Richard?"

"What have you got to lose? Besides," said Deirdre, tossing the holly in the gutter, "this only works with daisies. You'll have to wait until summer."

"I can't wait that long," said Hannah.

"I know you can't."

"Hannah Gold." Mr. Mandel consulted his list. "Your speech, please."

Hannah rose and walked to the front of the room. It was deathly quiet as she unlocked the violin case and rosined the bow. The noise of tuning the instrument seemed unnaturally loud and ugly to her, and Hannah's hands trembled as if this were an all-state audition. She held up the violin and pointed out the different parts of the instrument, then asked a volunteer to read the label inside. "Stradivarius," read Mary Short, and Hannah explained that there were thousands of imitation Stradivarius violins in existence. Her father had brought hers to Sotheby's in New York to be valued, and the expert told him they saw at least one imitation a week. "If mine was authentic," said Hannah, "I'd be at a private school in Switzerland." Everyone laughed.

Hannah began to feel more at ease. She had chosen a showy piece to play, and settled the violin under her chin. No trembling, no perspiring. In the front row Bobby grinned widely at her. She started playing, and the grin never left his face. Was he laughing at her? She played on, and the music took hold of her. She couldn't keep her shoulders from swaying. She couldn't keep the softness from her face. She finished and stood listening to the applause, beaming with happiness.

"Would someone be my guinea pig now?" said Hannah. A scattering of hands shot up, and avoiding Bobby's frantic waving, Hannah chose Richard. She showed him how to hold the violin, settling his chin on the chin rest. She could see a very slight stubble of beard on his face. His eyes were a pale blue. As she moved his arm across the strings she felt his sleek muscles move under his shirt. Richard was smiling now, and in the front row the smile was no longer on Bobby's face. Richard started gyrating his hips as if "Mary Had a Little Lamb" was heavy metal, and the class screamed and applauded loudly. Richard bowed, then made Hannah take a bow too. She sat down, grateful it was all over. Richard touched her hair as he passed her on the way to his seat. Hook, line, and sinker. Only Hannah was the one who was caught.

11

George and Hannah sat inside the smoky station, waiting to board the train to New York City. It was too cold to stand outside, and Hannah felt nauseated by the smell of stale smoke mingled with fresh perfume and overheated bodies. They sat on a bench, and Hannah leaned forward so her back wouldn't touch the graffiti-covered wall. George was beginning to get on her nerves: "Are you warm enough?" outside, and "I don't want you to catch cold—maybe you should undo your coat" inside.

Hannah sat, edgy, and took a book out of her purse. She couldn't concentrate and shut it quickly.

"Would you like me to buy you a newspaper?" George asked. "Or a magazine?"

"George, look after yourself," said Hannah. "You're driving me crazy." As soon as she'd said it she was sorry. George tried so hard—too hard. He reminded her of herself when she tried to be witty and ended up vulgar. She knew about trying too hard.

"I'm sorry," she said, and she squeezed George's arm. "I'll bet your parents do that. Hover over you. They say your parents are the prototype for your own behavior."

"I don't know about that mumbo jumbo," said George, "but my parents do look after my welfare, if that's what you mean."

"You're mad at me," said Hannah. "Come on, George." She pinched his cheek. "We'll have a great time. The Museum of Modern Art, and a walk in the sculpture garden and lunch, and maybe they'll be showing an old movie. I love the old movies."

"I like the new ones, myself," said George, but he softened a little when she took his hand. He leaned over and kissed her. There was nothing wrong with it. It wasn't wet or sloppy or hard, but she pulled away and busied herself rummaging through her purse for a mint.

The train pulled into the station, and the conductor called, "All aboard."

"That's what I like about these trains," whispered Hannah. "They still say 'All aboard,' like in the movies."

"In the old movies," said George, helping her up the steps.

She expected love to be like it was in the old Hollywood days. That was her problem. Passionate kisses where the faces don't move and nobody drools, and the boy doesn't keep trying to open your blouse. Oh, George was patient, but she felt as if she were treading water.

Holding her hand, George led Hannah down the aisle to an empty seat. She followed like a dog on a leash. When the train moved, she leaned her head on his shoulder and took a nap. George was good for that sort of thing.

Penn Station was teeming with people, and George pushed his way through the crowds to the subway quite expertly. Hannah was impressed as he waved aside a man who was hissing "Smoke, smoke" at them.

On the subway Hannah averted her eyes as a couple rubbed against each other. He held on to the pole, and she held on to him. She hoped George wouldn't get any ideas. She scanned the posters lining the wall of the car. A child's crude drawing of herself and her father in bed made her feel sick. FIGHT CHILD ABUSE. She turned away.

She watched the couple sitting opposite her. The woman was pregnant, and the man had his hand resting lightly on the woman's belly. His baby, his wife. Hannah couldn't imagine it. The rounded belly seemed like such a declaration of sex. She wished the man would take his hand away. She wished they would leave.

They reached the Fifty-third Street stop and followed the signs to the Museum of Modern Art. The city felt different to her. The menace was gone. Even the derelicts seemed cleaner, less threatening. And the paintings propped up against the wall before reaching the museum seemed fresher, racier than the artwork at the community center.

They entered the museum and George bought them tickets. He refused to allow Hannah to pay for anything. Only once, when he accepted an ice cream cone from her. She felt funny about it, and wondered where he got the money. Were his parents paying for his dates? Hannah had met George's mother once. She and George had picked her up at the beauty parlor where she got her hair done every week. She emerged with a bonnet of sprayed curls that stayed intact until the following appointment. She introduced George to all the beauticians, including the one who swept the floors and washed the hair. "My son Georgie," she said to the manicurist, beaming with pride. "My son Georgie," she said to the cashier. "Don't you have a daughter my Georgie's age?" she said loudly. Hannah stayed by the rubber plant, and George turned once, a "save me" look on his face, but he stayed dutifully by his mother's side. Hannah's mother got her hair trimmed every two months and came out unsprayed and smooth-capped. Did she brag to her hairdresser about her daughter? Hannah couldn't picture it. Maybe in a quieter way.

They threaded their way through the crowds gathered around Salvador Dali's dripping watch and into a room filled with Matisses. Hannah stood by a large painting of five dancing figures that took up most of an entire wall. *Dance,* it was called. She came here every year with her mother, and every year they sat on a bench and admired this picture. Hannah sat down. George sat next to her.

"You like this one?" he asked.

"I love it," said Hannah.

George approached the painting, and his finger hovered over an area of the canvas. "His brush dripped a little here. See?" He moved his finger to another spot. "And here. And look at this figure over here. She's all cockeyed. Why didn't he fix it?"

"I guess he didn't want to," said Hannah through her teeth. "He's painting emotion. The simplest way. You can't fix an emotion." She felt restless and turned away from the painting. She didn't want the blue sky, the pink bodies, the dance, dulled in any way. She didn't want to hate the painting.

The sculpture garden was closed, and Hannah pressed her nose against the glass, looking at the leafless trees and cold stone. Even Henry Moore's stone figures were cheerless.

"Lunch?" said George, and they found the end of the

line leading into the restaurant. Ahead of them was a well-dressed older woman holding the hand of another, younger, woman.

"I want a pizza," the younger woman said loudly. "Pizza, pizza," she chanted. Her face was blank, and she snapped a child's pink purse open and shut until the older woman took it from her.

"If they have it," she whispered.

Hannah wanted the young woman to get her pizza. She felt an urgency about it, as if she should run out and buy a piece for her if the restaurant had none. The older woman sighed and patted the arm of her friend, or was it her sister or daughter? What kind of life did the young woman have? Surely no telephone calls from boys, no flirting, no worrying about how fat she looked, the future, even. Just wanting pizza.

They moved along the lines, picking up tuna salad sandwiches and banana muffins. George carried the tray and arranged the silverware on it carefully.

"I don't like the mushy tomatoes on it!" cried the young woman, and before they even got to the cash register, the older woman was picking them off the pizza delicately with immaculately polished fingernails.

"It's such a shame," whispered Hannah to George. He looked questioningly at her.

Hannah motioned to the woman.

"The retarded girl?" he said, his face empty. "It happens. My cousin is retarded. Tell him to jump into a lake, and he will."

Hannah felt repelled by his matter-of-factness. "At least she got her pizza," she said.

George mussed her hair. "What are you talking about?"

After lunch, George held two tickets in the air and said, "It's showtime!" They went downstairs to the auditorium.

The room was packed. The museum was commemorating the films of George Stevens, and *Shane* was playing. Hannah showed George the program notes, but he waved them aside. "It's a cowboy movie," he said. "On TV all the time."

"It's a classic," hissed Hannah, and she felt like hitting him. The lights dimmed, and Alan Ladd rode onto the screen, the mysterious stranger. The man behind Hannah recited his lines word for word, but Hannah didn't care. And as the stranger fought man-to-man with Jean Arthur's husband, she wished that Jean could have them both. Then Shane rode off, bleeding, and the little boy called "Shaaaaaane, Shaaaane," so plaintively and "Mother wants you, I know she does, Shane. Come back!" so longingly that Hannah thought her heart would break.

She was quiet on the subway ride to Penn Station. She was silent as they waited for their train. George searched in his pockets for the tickets. "They've got to be here somewhere," he said.

"I can't go out with you anymore," said Hannah.

George looked at her in disbelief. "Because I've lost the tickets?" he said, his hands still searching.

"You're very nice, George," said Hannah, "but it isn't working out."

George slowly pulled his wallet out of his back pocket. He flipped through the cards and money, muttering "I know I have them." When he found the tickets, he handed one to Hannah and they boarded the train. This time George didn't help her up the steps, and Hannah walked down the aisle alone.

At the next orchestra rehearsal George moped around mournfully. At break time he stared at his fruit and cookies and didn't eat any. He polished his trumpet and blew spit out of the mouthpiece again and again.

After rehearsal, Hannah waited on the top steps and watched for her father's car. George slipped next to her and sat on the steps, cradling his head in his hands.

"Hi, George," she said softly.

"Why, Hannah?" he said, the words muffled in his coat. "What did I do?"

"You didn't do anything," she said. "I like you, George, I just didn't . . ." She chose her words carefully. "Feel anything for you."

George's cheek twitched as he looked at Hannah. "What the hell does that mean?" he said.

"I mean . . . when we kiss . . ." Hannah faltered. "When we kiss, I don't feel any spark."

"Fireworks are only in the movies," said George.

"Don't make this hard. There were other problems. But you're a nice person, George."

"You keep saying that. If I'm so nice, why are you breaking up with me?" It was George's turn to choose his words. "Maybe you're frigid," he said.

Hannah moved away, left the steps and the piteous creature on them. Where was her father? She peered into the darkness of the street, grateful when his car pulled up to the curb.

"That's why you don't feel anything," she heard him yell as she stepped into the car. "You're frigid!"

Maybe George was right. Maybe she was. But sitting next to her father in the warmth of the car it didn't matter. She switched on the radio and had to smile as she listened to "Girls Just Want to Have Fun." George was still sitting on the steps when they drove away.

12

It was a crisp, sunny Saturday morning, and Hannah didn't want to get out of bed. George could be right. Maybe she was frigid. If the right boy came along, maybe she wouldn't enjoy kissing him either. What if she finally got a date with Richard, and she felt the same way with him as she felt with George and Lance?

She didn't let herself look in the mirror. Nothing ever changed. Her hair was still long, brown, and straight, her hips large, her eyes small and green. Last summer she had worked in a factory for two weeks. Hundreds of dolls called Baby Catch a Ball rolled down the conveyor belt, and she put a little bonnet on every fourth doll. It was an ugly plastic baby, expressionless, and the only thing it could do was reach out its stiff arms and catch a ball. *Click, click,* like a steel trap, it held on to the ball. She hated the job and screwed up the courage to pretend she was fainting. . . . Oh, to get out of the hot, airless room, out of the din. The foreman took her arm and walked her to the nurse's office and made her sit down with her head between her legs. As he was leaving he turned to her. "Did anyone ever tell you that you have bedroom eyes?" he said. When she told her father, he made her quit the job. He told her she should never have been hired in the first place, she was underage. Hannah had never seen her father so angry.

Bedroom eyes. She liked the sound of it. It made her feel like a romantic heroine, carried away by the swashbuckling hero to his castle. She would have cleavage, and violet eyes, and boyish hips.

Being swept away no longer felt like part of the picture. Sweeping away George was all that had happened. Passion was a myth. Kissing was a bore. Either that, or George was right.

Hannah pushed back the covers and let the cold air hit her. Saturday morning meant an eleven o'clock violin lesson. She wasn't in the mood. She threw on a bathrobe and went downstairs to the kitchen. She hated the sight of the framed ripe tomatoes and crisp, round peas. They were too cheery. A dark, rainy day would have suited her. Classical music was playing on the radio. Hannah switched it quickly to a rock station and looked at her mother, cooking oatmeal. She dared her to complain.

"Don't forget you have a lesson this morning," said her mother mildly.

"How could I forget?" said Hannah, munching on a spoonful of cornflakes she had poured.

"Are you seeing George tonight?" asked her mother.

"We broke up," said Hannah. She stirred the cereal idly.

"That's why you're such a bear this morning," said her mother.

"I'm not a bear, and it's been over a week now," said Hannah. "I broke it off, not George."

"He was a little bossy," said her mother.

"And Daddy's not bossy?" snapped Hannah.

Her mother put down the cereal spoon. "Honey, you'll meet someone else. Just enjoy your friends, and do what makes you happy."

"I don't know what makes me happy. I just don't feel anything for boys." Hannah mushed the cereal savagely. "I don't even like being kissed."

Her mother sprinkled raisins on her oatmeal. "You didn't like the boys, so why would you like being kissed by them?"

"Maybe I'm frigid," said Hannah, and she threw the leftover cornflakes into the garbage can.

Her mother poured some coffee. "You haven't eaten anything, Hannah. Sit down and let me make you some toast."

"No, thanks," said Hannah, but she sat down again.

"You're not frigid," her mother said, facing Hannah. "It takes two people who like each other very much, who accept each other, to make a good relationship."

"Like you and Daddy," Hannah said sarcastically. "The perfect couple."

"A good relationship doesn't just happen. Daddy and I have to work at it. The same thing goes for sex and kissing." Her mother took a deep breath. "The boys were not right for you. And when you meet someone you really like, you'll feel differently." She reached over and placed a hand over Hannah's. "Believe me," she said.

"Maybe just a piece of cinnamon toast," said Hannah. Her mother put a slice of raisin bread into the toaster.

"When I was a little older than you—I think it was my freshman year at Hunter College—I felt the same way." She looked around as if she were about to divulge classified information. She said in a low voice, "I was convinced I was a lesbian."

"A what?" said Hannah, and she started to laugh.

"Just what I said." Her mother spread butter on the toast and sprinkled it with cinnamon sugar. "That sort of thing was around then too, you know. And then I met your father." She smiled. "The rest, as they say, is history."

The doorbell startled them, and Hannah jumped up from the table. "Your toast!" said her mother. Hannah grabbed it and ran up the stairs calling back, "Tell him I'll be down in a minute!" She threw on her clothes and took her violin case out of the closet.

When she came back down again, her mother was hanging up Mr. Kreutzer's coat. Hannah hugged her hard and said, "Thanks." Then she walked into the living room, where Mr. Kreutzer waited, for her violin lesson.

13

*M*r. Kreutzer was a dapper man, and he always arrived smelling heavily of cologne. He was a second-rate fiddle player but a patient teacher, who played first chair in the community orchestra and had taught in the public schools for years. A few years back his wife had died, and Hannah remembered a year of melancholy marked by the somberness of the music he brought her. He left the school system shortly after. "I can't teach little brats whose mothers bribe them to practice," he told Hannah. It alarmed her. Some days she felt like her mother was a little dog yapping "Practice, practice" at her heels. She longed to shake the little dog away, throw it out the window. Instead she practiced every day, and Mr. Kreutzer rewarded her diligence with choice duets and beautiful solo pieces that he would pull out of his battered briefcase after the dull exercises were completed. On good days they hugged when they were finished, and today's lesson was a good one. Hannah said good-bye and joined her parents in the kitchen. "I smell like Old Spice!" she said, and her parents laughed.

The telephone rang, and her mother answered it. Her

greeting was warm and her eyes took on a brightness. Hannah exchanged glances with her father. "Grandma," he said.

They listened. "You're not doing anything today?" There was a hesitation in Hannah's mother's voice now. "We thought we might go to a museum," she said, glancing at Hannah's father.

"Grandma is giving your mother the guilt now," he said, "and your mother just bought it." Her mother's eyes narrowed, and she spoke into the receiver. "Hold on." She cupped her hand over the mouthpiece. "How about putting off the museum and visiting Grandma and Grandpa instead?" she said.

"What a surprise!" said Mr. Gold. Hannah burst into laughter.

"I'll get you two later," her mother said, and she spoke into the telephone. "We'll see you in about an hour. We'll bring some cake." She laughed, and crinkles sprang into the corners of her eyes. "So we'll all get fat together."

As long as Hannah could remember, crossing the George Washington Bridge signaled their arrival to Grandma's. The lobby of the old building had the same plastic flowers in the same dusty gravel, the hallways smelled of years of solid cooking—pot roasts and chicken soup, blintzes and stuffed cabbage—and there was Grandma, laughing in the doorway. Grandpa was the quiet one, blue eyes peering over her shoulder, and he moved slowly with his cane. He was impeccably dressed in a suit and tie although he hadn't worked since his stroke nine years before. Hannah kissed him first. He smelled faintly of lemon, called her his Hannahleh, and kissed her back.

Grandma was in her element, dishing out soup and ordering Grandpa to hang up coats and get the children soda. Hannah's mother was immediately one of the children, and she smiled when Grandma blatantly gave her the biggest knaidlach and the plumpest piece of white chicken. "Cream soda for my little girl," said Grandpa, setting the glass before his daughter. Hannah's claim to the chicken was always the drumstick, and she wondered how their favorite foods were always readily available here, bestowed on them like kings and queens. They ate as if they'd be fasting for days to come. After coffee and cake, Hannah went into her grandparents' bedroom and, taking a novel from Grandma's bookcase, lay on the big bed. Everywhere there were framed pictures of family, living and dead—on the walls, on dressers, taped on mirrors, propped on lamp stands. Grandpa looked aristocratic in his wedding picture, with a monocle and silver-tipped cane, and Grandma was an exotic flower with a cascade of white blossoms at her bosom.

It was in this room that Jean and Hannah had found the stash of dirty books behind the historical novels, books like *Candy,* which they read aloud, devouring the steamy sex scenes. They hid them away quickly when the door creaked open or when someone entered the nearby bathroom. The grownups could talk for hours, and Hannah and Jean would read, eyes popping, screaming with laughter. Once, when Hannah acted out a scene, her tongue touched Jean's accidentally, and they screeched so loudly that their mother came running. "I got my finger caught in the drawer," gasped Hannah, and her mother looked at them suspiciously but was pulled back to the dining room by the sound of her mother and father and husband laughing and talking. She shut the door firmly and Jean screamed, "What finger? What drawer?" and she stuck out her tongue until they were hysterical all over again.

It was quiet now without Jean, and Hannah sat up and pulled open the dresser drawers, discovering the same trinkets she'd played with as a child. The red ruby brooches and diamond necklaces that looked so real when she was young looked like cheap costume jewelry now. The fur collars and beaded sweaters, the array of colored scarves that ladies wore—silk, polyester, cashmere, acrylic, the drawer was bursting with them. A small box of trinkets was marked ROZZIE, Grandma's first sister to go, "the pretty one" the family called her, just as Aunt Esther was "the foxy one," the one who had five husbands. Grandma was "the smart one," but when Hannah got older her grandmother told her, "I always wanted to be the pretty one." In a flash she saw Grandma as a young girl. She felt close to her, much closer than flesh and blood, as if she could see a glimpse of herself in Grandma's eyes.

Hannah no longer looked for dirty books. In fact, it looked as though Grandma didn't read them anymore. She knew Grandma still slept with Grandpa in the big bed, because she remembered her mother telling her father in the car, "She says Papa still gives her a tumble in bed. Can you imagine?" Hannah pretended she was asleep in the back seat, but it was a revelation to her. Her father replied, "Life doesn't stop when you get old, you know," and her mother said she knew that, but it was hard to think of your own parents that way.

Hannah agreed. She remembered walking into her parents' bedroom one morning without knocking. She caught a split-second glimpse of her parents' naked bodies locked together and heard her father yell "Shit!" so loudly that she shut the door and left the house. She hardly knew what she had seen, perhaps only covers flapping in the air, but from her father's tone of voice, his choice of word, she knew that she had interrupted something very secret and very private.

Now she lay on the bed, not reading. Her grandfather came in and sat down in the only armchair and said, "So how is my Hannahleh?"

She told him about George, without the frigid part, and finished by telling him how hopeless she was with boys. Her grandfather snorted and said she couldn't be worse than he had been. "I was forty-two when I married your grandmother, and a green apple until then. Grandma taught me everything. You'll meet a boy and you'll teach each other." Then he took out a clean white handkerchief and dabbed his eyes. "She made me laugh," he said. "That's how she won me. She made me laugh." He looked up at Hannah, and his eyes were blue crystal. "She still does, you know." He pushed himself up from the chair and steadied himself with his cane as he walked over to her and kissed the top of her head. When he had left the room, she lay back on the pillow. The scent of lemon was on it.

A week later her grandfather died. Hannah's mother heard the news over the telephone, and she made the most terrible sounds. Animal sounds. Her face crumpled and her mouth opened and closed, and Hannah heard her say, "Oh, Mother, oh, Mother," again and again. That's when Hannah knew he was dead—not watching her mother cry but hearing her say "Oh, Mother."

Jean flew in from college the next day, and they drove

to the funeral parlor, the four of them, talking about Grandpa on the way. Jean said, "I remember the way Grandma called him, so annoyed at him, 'Julius, Julius, what are you doing?' and Grandpa would laugh and call out her name, 'Oy, oy, Molly, Molly, what's the matter?' until she'd laugh, too." Their mother nodded her head and told their father to keep his eyes on the road.

They stood with Grandma and greeted everyone who came to pay their respects. Names of relatives were whispered to Hannah and Jean as they approached. Their faces were smudged with bright lipstick imprints, and vague memories of earlier meetings came flooding back. Sweet Aunt Fanny, who never criticized anyone, snappy Aunt Fanny, who called a spade a spade. Once at a wedding Grandma said, "Wasn't the bride beautiful?" and Aunt Fanny said, "A face like a hatchet." Uncle Gus, whose cigar butts were always found floating in the toilet when he visited. And Uncle Harry, the prince of the family, so surrounded by adoring sisters that he never married, but he pulled quarters from his nieces' ears and captured their noses until it was time to give them back.

The rabbi spoke of Grandpa, but it was not the Grandpa she knew. Grandma, standing between Hannah's parents, sobbed and nodded. Then the rabbi said, "Jules Goodman, your family and friends will mourn your passing," and there were murmurs of "Julius, Julius" as the mourners corrected him. But the rabbi kept on, and "Jules" and "Julius" filled the air, until Hannah started to laugh silently, her shoulders shaking up and down, and then Jean caught it and couldn't stop herself. Then the hiccups started, and Hannah heard sweet Aunt Fanny whisper from behind them, "The poor children are crying," and their laughter strangled them once more.

Afterward, they drove Grandma to the cemetery—she didn't want a limousine. "I want my family," she said, "nothing fancy." Hannah sat next to her, listening to Grandma say "My poor Julius" as she sighed and patted Hannah's knee.

"Do you remember," said Hannah, "when we decided to have a picnic at the park your friend recommended?"

"Which park was that?" said Jean, watching Grandma's face.

Grandma's face was blank. Hannah went on. "Grandpa had just had his stroke, and we needed a park that wasn't hilly so that Grandpa could walk from the car."

"I don't remember that," said Jean.

Grandma threw up her hands. "I do. Grandpa laughed so hard I thought he would have another stroke. It was Mount Hebron, and Bertha gave me directions and never asked me what for. And it was a cemetery!"

"And Ben and Grandpa wanted to stay there," said Hannah's mother, "because they were hungry."

"Meshuganas!" said Grandma.

"Tuna fish never tasted so good," said Hannah's father, smacking his lips. "And Grandpa enjoyed himself. Fresh air and food that wasn't from the hospital."

Grandma smiled, and then her face clouded over. "My poor Julius," she said. "Did he know how much I loved him? Forty years of fighting. Did he know?"

"You made him happy, Mother. You were a good wife. You took care of him when he was sick."

"My sharp tongue," said Grandma, shaking her head as

if to rid herself of the memories. "The day before he died I hollered at him. A dish he broke, I don't know what."

"Mom," said Hannah's mother. "He loved you. You loved him. Rest easy, Mom."

"You always made him laugh, Grandma," said Hannah. "Even if you yelled. He said that's how you won him."

"Won him?" Grandma looked up. "He was the prize. Gentle. A good man. He never complained. I did all the complaining."

"He wouldn't have had you any other way, Mother."

"Once he left me," said Grandma. "Did you know that?" Hannah's mother shook her head.

"He said he couldn't do it. Support a wife and two children, and one on the way." Grandma's shoulders slumped.

"What happened, Grandma?" said Hannah.

"He was away a whole day, with a suitcase yet." Grandma pulled back her shoulders and straightened her hat. "He came back. He put his arms around me, and he grabbed the children, too, and told us he missed us. He didn't know what had come over him." Grandma fumbled in her purse for a handkerchief. "And when I lost the baby he cried his eyes out. He said God was punishing him for even thinking of leaving. I told him it wasn't so. But he cried and cried."

"I remember that," Hannah's mother said softly. "I never saw Papa cry before. He sat in the armchair in your bedroom, and we could hear him through the walls. Joseph and I pushed the door open. We could see him, but he waved us away."

They approached the cemetery. Hannah's father held Grandma's arm as they walked toward the plot. When Grandma saw the coffin she cried out and flung away his arm. Hannah held her breath as they lowered the box into the hole. Grandma was handed a shovel. She looked at it as if it were a foreign object and stood stiffly until her daughter helped her scoop up some earth and guided her hand to sprinkle in onto the casket. It scattered with a patter of sound. One at a time, other friends and relatives shoveled earth onto the box. As Hannah took the shovel Grandma shrieked and threw herself at the grave, the veil she wore flying and her pocketbook pitching into the dirt. Hannah's father and Uncle Harry sprang forward to catch her. Grandma struggled and sobbed, "I want to be with him." Hannah took Jean's hand, and they stood watching as their mother put her arms around Grandma and led her away. This is death, thought Hannah. Grandpa is in the ground, and Grandma will sleep alone tonight. No more prune juice and borscht especially made for Grandpa. No more laughter as Grandma does a little dance in the kitchen, spoon in hand. Why was everyone saying poor Grandpa? Poor everybody left behind.

They drove Grandma back home. Pots of steaming coffee were perking and trays of food were laid out on the table. People scooped whitefish and cream cheese and lox onto fresh bagels, and suddenly it was life again, a party, not death. Hannah ate hungrily, and even Grandma had coffee and nibbled on a piece of rugalach. The apartment reverberated with the sounds of talking and laughing, and Jean and Hannah went into the bedroom and sat on the floor, leaning against the coat-covered bed.

"I don't want to die," said Hannah. "It's so weird. You get married and have a family and die."

"You die whether you have a family or not," said Jean.

"Will I ever meet someone I like, who'll like me?" said Hannah, stroking a fur coat behind her.

"You'll meet someone, marry him, and die," said Jean.

Hannah looked shocked, and Jean laughed. "I'm only kidding," she said, putting a man's hat on Hannah's head.

"Yick!" said Hannah. "That might be Uncle Herman's, and he has dandruff!" She flipped the hat like a Frisbee across the bed. "Do you think Grandma will remarry?"

Jean shrugged. "Who knows? Women outnumber men, and the men die earlier."

"Men still have it easier," said Hannah. "They can pick and choose. Would Grandma know how to flirt?"

"In her own way, I guess. She's not Aunt Esther, but she's funny, and a good cook, too. Old men care about that." Jean laughed. "I make great scrambled eggs. They'll have to settle for that."

"Really?" said Hannah. "You don't care if you can't cook? Grandma says that the way to a man's heart is through his stomach."

"Not anymore," said Jean. "I was at Sam's the other day, and he said he was in the mood for French toast. I wasn't sure if I knew how to make it, so he showed me. I told him he made such great French toast, he should make it for me from now on."

Hannah was making French toast in her head now, with great seriousness. Did you add milk to the eggs? Cinnamon or nutmeg? What if she burned it in front of him? In front of whom? Grandpa's grave loomed suddenly, and Grandma pitching forward. She felt desperate.

"How do I keep it from getting soggy?" How short was the distance between making French toast for a boy and death?

Jean's voice was gentle. "Stale bread. That's the secret. Don't worry about it."

"All I can do is play the violin." She felt as if she were choking. "The way to a man's heart is not through the violin." Hannah's hand touched the ugly head of a chinchilla, or was it a mink, and she flung it away.

"You know what?" Jean sat up. "When I want friends— I mean, when I'm lonely and the neediness is written all over my face, they run the other way. Like I have a disease. When I'm happy—you know, jogging or doing what I like to do, they all come running. It's funny."

"I guess," said Hannah. "But you can't suddenly get happy."

"You'll meet boys soon enough," said Jean. "Remember, I'm your older and wiser sister. Having a boyfriend isn't everything. Have a good time with your friends. If Deirdre is busy with Pete, see Nancy and Mary. How is Deirdre, by the way?"

"Still blond and bubbly," said Hannah.

"As opposed to you, I suppose. Brunette and bummed out," Jean said, pinching her.

Hannah laughed, and she wasn't strangling anymore. "Let me be a little miserable today, okay?"

When they left that night, Hannah opened the closet door and pulled out her jacket. It was next to Grandpa's heavy overcoat, and she buried her face in the coat. It smelled of lemon. She put on her jacket and went to kiss her grandmother. Grandma's kiss pricked her cheek, a mole with tiny thistles that had tickled her for as long as she could remember. The prickly kiss and the lemon scent. She didn't want to forget them.

14

*H*annah was glad to be back at school, away from caskets and funerals. She hung her jacket in her locker and grabbed her gym clothes.

"Was it awful?" asked Deirdre.

"Grandma tried to throw herself into the grave," said Hannah. She sniffed the white shirt. "These gym clothes smell terrible."

"Sprinkle them with baby powder." Deirdre fished in her purse and handed Hannah a container. "Your poor grandmother." She put her arm around Hannah. "I'm so glad you're back. I missed you. I told everyone why you were out. How do you feel?"

"I feel sort of different," said Hannah. "It makes you think, when you're that close to death. About what's important."

"What's important?" said Deirdre, sniffing her own gym clothes.

"Family. And love."

"Maybe your family. I don't know about mine. Speaking of love, look who just walked around the corner."

Richard Milliken swung open his locker and called to Hannah, "Sorry about your grandmother."

"Grandfather," said Hannah. "Thanks."

"You missed my speech," said Richard. "Obedience training for your dog. It was pretty good. I brought Trigger in, and she showed off her tricks. A regular show-biz performer. Everyone loved it."

"We all barked our appreciation," said Deirdre.

"Funny."

"Sounds great," said Hannah. They walked to Mr. Mandel's class. "Who's up today?"

Deirdre rolled her eyes. "Enid is showing us how to wrap a present. I don't remember who else."

"Just what I need," said Richard. "Now I can run out and get a job at the nearest shopping mall."

They took their seats, and Hannah felt a familiar tap on her shoulder.

"Sorry to hear about your grandfather," said Bobby. "Was he sick or something?"

"He had a stroke a long time ago," said Hannah. "But he was doing just fine. I'd just seen him. It was out of the blue."

"My dad died last year," said Bobby. "A heart attack. My father the jogger. It was a real shock. He went out and walked the dog, came back, and my mother found him on the kitchen floor. There was water all over the place. I guess he was getting it for the dog."

Hannah didn't know what to say. His father. She couldn't imagine it. Her father dead. She wanted to find him and hug him, rub the top of his bald head. "How awful," she said.

"I miss him," said Bobby. "I mean, we watched the games together, we talked. But you took it for granted it would go on forever."

"I know," said Hannah. She could see Grandpa laughing now, and tears sprang to her eyes. "I'm afraid I'll forget him," she said.

"But you've got the memories." said Bobby.

Mr. Mandel took out his list and called out Mary Plunkett's name. Mary hurried to the front of the room, clutching a fishing tackle box.

"The topic of my speech," began Mary, scattering pots and brushes and sticks on the table, "is how to put on makeup." She called for a female volunteer, and several girls raised their hands.

"No fair, Margie, Jessica—put your hands down," said Mary. "I need someone who doesn't wear much makeup."

Hannah willed herself to be called. It was the chance she had been waiting for. What was it they had learned in class? *Carpe diem.* Seize the day.

Hannah nearly jumped out of her chair when she heard her name. Someone, that rotten new Hannah, that brave new Hannah, was pushing her out of the chair and forcing her to walk to the front of the room, twenty-six pairs of eyes glued to her as she braced herself on the strategically placed chair. She mentally fastened her seat belt. Thank God she had no pimples. Thank God she was alive.

Mary looked solemn. "Hannah," she said, "I am not a dentist."

Hannah started to laugh. Mary dabbed a damp sponge in foundation, and her hand hovered above Hannah's laughing face. "Relax," she said. Hannah relaxed her features into a smooth mask. "Shadow and contour is everything," said Mary. "I'm lucky with Hannah. She has great cheekbones." She brushed Hannah's cheeks, chin, and forehead with the sponge. "If you use a light dusting powder, before and after you apply your makeup, it makes for a finer finish." She dusted on some powder. "And if you choose an eyeliner that complements your eye color, it will enhance your eyes." Mary applied some purple liner under Hannah's eyes. "See? Her eyes are green, and the purple emphasizes them. Just a little mascara. Hannah has very dramatic eyebrows, so we'll leave them alone." She brushed on some pink blush, then dusted on more powder. Hannah sneezed, and Mary laughed. "It's best to go easy on the powder, so as not to asphyxiate the victim." Mary pointed to Hannah. "Move over, Christie Brinkley," she said. "Finished."

"You oughta be in pictures," called out Bobby, and the class applauded. There were even a few whistles.

"Hey, green eyes," said Richard as she sat down. Hannah slipped a mirror out of her purse and sneaked a look. Not bad. Not bad at all.

"Enid Grove," called Mr. Mandel.

Enid fumbled with paper, tape, scissors, and ribbon, and they learned how to wrap a present. At least some of them did. Hannah was thinking that she'd stop at the drugstore and pick up some purple eyeliner.

Late that night Hannah practiced putting on makeup, a jumble of tubes and containers on her bed as she struggled to get the same effect that Mary had so easily achieved. Forget the foundation, unless she had pimples. The purple eyeliner gave her trouble, until she remembered that Mary had suggested a wet Q-tip to remove rough edges. She quietly slipped into the bathroom and opened the medicine cabinet slowly so that it wouldn't squeak. Lately her mother went to bed early. "I'm so tired," she told Hannah after supper. She looked as if she never slept at all.

Tonight they were awake. She could hear her parents talking, a low rumble through the walls. Her father's voice got louder. "I'm dying!" he cried, and Hannah's heart leaped in terror, but she knew he wasn't dying. "You're killing me," he said. Her mother's voice was a sob. "I can't help it, Ben. You have to give me more time." Hannah held her hands over her ears, but she left a space because she had to hear, like in a scary movie when you peer through your fingers at the horror. "I need a woman," said her father. "I need love." Hannah left the bathroom and shut her bedroom door. She wanted to cement it closed, stuff the cracks with newspaper, remove the doorknob. She swept the makeup aside and got under the covers, pressing her face into the pillow, pulling up the ends against her ears. Finally she fell asleep, purple rings around her eyes, violet smudges on the pillow.

15

*D*eirdre's house was ablaze with Christmas lights. Hannah was staying there for the weekend while her parents helped her grandmother pack up Grandpa's things.

"Dad always overdoses on the lights," said Deirdre. "Every year my mother wants one tree with blue lights—she thinks it looks classier. And Dad promises. Then he starts putting them up—and this is what we get." The roof was a web of colored lights and each of the four spruce trees in front of the house was a different color. Two red-nosed reindeer stood guard, and a Santa Claus seemed to balance precariously by the chimney.

"Wonderland," said Deirdre. "And with their usual Christmas spirit, my parents aren't talking."

Hannah's parents weren't exactly talking either. Her mother was quiet at breakfast this morning, and her father had already left for work. What's happening, she thought silently, watching her mother stir the oatmeal. Tell me what's the matter. She couldn't bring herself to ask.

Supper at the Kileys' was a silent affair, too. Mr. Kiley said to Deirdre, "Please tell your mother to pass the French fries." Deirdre's mother sat stone-faced, barely touching her food. Deirdre ate hungrily.

"How is school, Hannah?" Mrs. Kiley asked brightly, ignoring the request for French fries. "What was the topic of your speech?"

"I demonstrated the violin," said Hannah, swallowing another French fry. Her mother never served them—too much fat, she warned, but Deirdre's house was junk-food heaven. White bread and doughnuts, too, and Hannah loved it.

"You're so talented," said Deirdre's mother, nibbling on her hamburger. "Our Deirdre doesn't have any talents. Unless you count her talent for driving me crazy, right, Deirdre?"

"Sure, that's right." Deirdre poured herself some soda and said, "Another gourmet meal, Mom. I think I'll go throw up."

Hannah look at Mr. Kiley. Her father would never allow her or Jean to talk to their mother that way. She recalled the lectures on respecting your parents that went on and on, until her mother came to their rescue. "They get the message, Ben," she'd say, and Hannah and Jean would run to their mother and say they were sorry. Maybe staying with the Kileys was a mistake. Maybe meals with Deirdre should remain afternoon snacks.

Mrs. Kiley pushed back her chair, banging it against the wall. Her husband kept eating without looking up.

"What am I, a doormat? I cook and clean and chauffeur, not a word of thanks, and then I'm supposed to give you a culinary masterpiece for supper. You've got another thing coming, young lady." Mrs. Kiley whipped the plates off the table and threw them into the sink. "You can start by cleaning up. You'd better wash out that foul mouth of yours while you're at it."

"No way," said Deirdre, pushing back from the table. "You get up late, there's never anything to eat in the house, and you're always on my back." Deirdre's eyes were blazing and she stood, head forward, like an attack dog. "And you never have one good word to say about me."

Hannah held her breath, her eyes glued to the half-eaten hamburger in front of her. She was ready to bolt.

"Apologize to your mother," said Mr. Kiley, standing up at last.

"What about you?" Deirdre answered. "Suddenly you're her best friend. Why don't you tell her not to speak to me that way?"

Mrs. Kiley spoke up. "When you learn to act like a human being, we'll treat you like one. And you watch that tone of voice. My father would have taken the strap to me if I'd spoken to him that way." She pushed her hair out of her eyes. "I ought to do it myself. If your father wasn't so mealy-mouthed—"

"Shut up, Ethel." Mr. Kiley pulled the tab on a can of beer. It spilled over his hand. "Damn," he said, shaking the excess into the sink.

"This house smells like a brewery!" cried Mrs. Kiley shrilly, and she stormed out of the room.

"Do me a favor, Deirdre," said her father.

"What?" she said, looking down at the linoleum.

"Do the dishes," he said, and walked out of the kitchen.

"Does that sort of thing happen a lot?" asked Hannah, stacking the dried plates on a corner of the kitchen table. She had never seen a table filled with so much clutter . . .

bars of soap, pads of paper, letters, advertisements, boxes of bobby pins, pots and pans, jars of jam, empty bottles, assorted lids, stacks of coupons, packages of soy sauce and duck sauce and countless Chinese tea bags, even a bowl of chopsticks.

"My mother doesn't throw anything away," said Deirdre. "Sure, it happens all the time. She thinks I'm here on this earth just to torture her." Deirdre wrung the water out of the dishcloth as if she were wringing someone's neck. "She hates me. I can't do anything right."

"I'm sure she doesn't hate you," said Hannah. It occurred to her that tonight she didn't want to be Deirdre. She looked at Mrs. Kiley's clutter and saw her mother's gleaming white-tiled kitchen table, clear of everything except a pot of African violets.

"She doesn't hate me?" Deirdre spread the dishcloth over the dish rack to dry. "Then why can't she say anything good about me?" She switched off the kitchen light. "If it wasn't for Pete, I don't know what I'd do."

Hannah didn't want to go to the party.

"I told Pete you were coming," said Deirdre, "and he'll be insulted if you don't." Deirdre held up a red off-the-shoulder sweater. "What do you think?"

"Daring," said Hannah, "but okay if you have a boy-friend. Why would he be insulted?"

"He'll think you don't want to meet his friends. I'll wear it, then." Deirdre swung her head down and gathered her hair into a ponytail. "Up or down?"

"Down. It'll cover some of that shoulder." Hannah shifted some of the clothes piled on Deirdre's bed and made a space for herself. She wished she had the nerve to wear bare shoulders. Just one bare shoulder. "I have nothing to wear."

"I'll find something for you. What about my green blouse and your good jeans?" Deirdre waded through the stack of blouses.

"I hate when you do that, because you know I couldn't fit into any of your clothes." Hannah sighed. "I always feel like Laurel and Hardy when I'm with you."

"Which one am I?" said Deirdre.

"I don't know. I'm the fat one who's always mad."

"And I'm the skinny one who's always crying?" Deirdre laughed. "Around my mother I'm mad and crying, so I could be either one."

"I'm a giant next to you."

"Would you cut it out? If you must know, Pete says you have a nice figure, and that you hide it." Deirdre painted some lip gloss on her mouth. "Mary says if you put gloss on your bottom lip only, your lips look fuller. I say they look half done." She examined her mouth, then looked sideways at Hannah. "I'm not jealous or anything, but I wish you'd stop putting yourself down."

She wished she could. It was like a bad habit she'd gotten into that she couldn't stop. She felt funny that Pete had noticed her figure. He'd never even looked at her. And Deirdre was right. This morning when she complimented Enid on a sweater she was wearing, Enid screwed up her face and said, "This? I look like Miss Piggy in it." It was supposed to be funny, but Hannah had this crawling familiar feeling. She sounded like that, and it was awful.

They watched television and waited for Pete to pick them up. A game show was blaring, and Mrs. Kiley was shouting out the answers to the questions. She looked so happy, crying, "Take the car, the car. Or the cruise. Take the cruise!" Hannah had never seen her look so happy. Mr. Kiley was staring out the window into the darkness, a beer can in his hand. When Pete honked his horn, he said dully, "Home by one o'clock."

One o'clock? thought Hannah. An eternity. What if the party was awful? She remembered that the next morning she had her violin lesson, too. Why hadn't she gone with her parents?

Pete honked insistently and Deirdre didn't bother to close her coat. She opened the car door and slid next to him. Hannah slipped in beside Deirdre.

"Hey," Pete said, and he bent to kiss Deirdre. He tapped Hannah on the shoulder. "Hey," he said. Was that the only word in his vocabulary? Hannah smiled and leaned her forehead against the cold windowpane. It was going to be a long evening.

Tim Danson's parents weren't home, and music blared as Pete opened the door. Inside it was hot and smoky, and Hannah could see a blur of couples slow-dancing in the dark.

"Drink?" said Pete, a six-pack of beer under his arm. Hannah shook her head, but Deirdre took one.

"I thought you didn't drink beer," whispered Hannah as she watched Deirdre tilt back her head and take a long swig.

"Pete taught me to like it," said Deirdre.

"Great," said Hannah. He was a teacher now, this boy/ex-convict who spoke in monosyllables. What did Deirdre see in him?

"Try it," said Deirdre, handing her the can. "After a while it doesn't taste so bad."

"Listen to her," said Pete, "the big drinker. The first time she drank two whole cans, she puked all over my car."

"Maybe that should have taught her something," said Hannah. She hated it that she sounded prim and proper, but she rushed on. "It obviously doesn't agree with her."

"You're a barrel of laughs," said Pete, raising an eyebrow. Hannah saw Deirdre motion to her to stop whatever she was doing. She headed for the safest corner and sat down on the sofa. She planted her feet. This was her Monopoly square. She would go directly to Jail and lose one turn. She would not take a drink if she didn't want to. She would stay here forever.

A boy sat down next to her. His eyes looked glazed, and perspiration ran down the side of his face. "Long hair," he said. Hannah leaned away from the boy and he leaned closer. "What sign are you?" he slurred, a glass lurching in his hand and liquid spilling onto the carpet.

"Taurus," said Hannah, looking around.

"The bull," said the boy. "Are you full of bull?"

"You're drunk," said Hannah. She wanted him banished from her safe square. She wanted him gone. She rose to leave.

"She says I'm drunk," shouted the boy, and he leaned heavily against her. Hannah was afraid that if she moved away he'd fall flat on his face. In the movies someone would make him a cup of coffee.

She moved away anyway, and the boy fell back on the arm of the sofa and slid to the floor.

"You've got quite a wallop!" he said, and Hannah looked around to see if anyone had heard him. She spotted a familiar face, and he was coming toward her. Hannah felt like running away.

Steve Talbot gestured toward the sprawling figure. "I see you had quite an effect on him," he said. "Rich told me all about you."

"What did he tell you?" Hannah said, wishing she could think of a wisecrack.

"Oh, that you don't miss a trick." He held out a bowl of potato chips, and Hannah shook her head. "What are you doing here, anyway?" he asked.

"I'm here with Deirdre," said Hannah. She wished Steve hadn't seen her. Now he would tell Richard that she was sitting all alone.

"And she's here with Pete." Steve shook his head. "What a waste."

"You don't like Pete?" said Hannah. They had something in common.

Steve shrugged. "He's a loser. And she's kind of cute. She sent me a note in English, you know. 'Is it true blondes have more fun?' Cute. And then she started going with him." Steve ran his hand through his hair. "Her loss."

"I'm staying at her house for the weekend." Hannah made a face. "Have you ever met her parents?"

"Mrs. Kiley is a bitch on wheels," said Steve. "I heard her in the supermarket, battling it out over the ice cream counter with the old man. A divorce lawyer's dream."

"Do you think so? They might be better off divorced." Hannah relaxed a little, and she took a handful of potato chips.

"That kind of marriage goes on forever. Rich's parents are like that. His father freezes them out and his mother screams her head off. Poor Rich."

"I read somewhere that if your parents have a good marriage, you're more likely to have one." Hannah bit her lip and wished the remark away. She sounded like such a nerd, she wanted to vomit. Steve didn't seem to notice. His eyes were on Deirdre, hands on her hips, chin jutting. Definitely the attack dog position.

Deirdre's voice was rising, and Hannah could hear snatches of what she was saying.

"You're crazy . . . he never put a hand on me." She stalked off and Pete went after her.

"He's high as a kite," said Steve. "Like I said. She picked a loser. See you later."

He left Hannah alone. She took a deep breath. There seemed to be a lull in the dancing, and something was being passed around, hand to hand. She shook her head when the joint reached her. She didn't want to smoke it, and the idea of all those lips on that makeshift cigarette made her feel sick. It would circle around and reach her once more if she didn't move.

Pete was suddenly breathing down her neck, a beer can in his hand.

"Hey, schoolteacher, loosen up. You're not in violin class now."

"I'm fine," said Hannah, looking around wildly for Steve.

"Take a hit then," he said, and she shook her head.

"Where's Deirdre?" Hannah said, her voice sounding strange to her.

"Bawling in the bathroom." Pete put his face close to her and she could smell the beer on his breath. "I caught her messing around with someone else, and I told her she could walk home." Pete lifted the beer can and pressed it to Hannah's lips. "I like schoolteachers. Have a little sip."

"No, thank you," she said, pushing the can away. It splashed wildly onto her cheek and ran down her neck. Tears sprang to her eyes, and Pete caught her wrist as she tried to walk by him.

"What's with you?" he said, and pulled her toward him.

"I have to go to the bathroom." Hannah jerked her arm away and ran down the hall. Where was the bathroom, anyway? She knocked hard on the nearest closed door. "Deirdre," she called out. "Are you in there?"

Water was running and she heard a muffled reply. "I'll be out in a minute."

"It's me, Hannah. Let me in!"

Deirdre opened the door, dabbing her nose and eyes with toilet paper.

"He thinks I'm flirting with Tim. All I was doing was talking, and Pete turns into a maniac." Tears ran down her cheeks, and streaks of black mascara ringed her eyes. "What am I going to do?"

"He's a jerk," said Hannah. "Let's just go. Can we call your father or something?"

"My father? Are you kidding?" Deirdre sniffled and turned on the cold water. She held a folded piece of paper towel under the water and blotted it. Then she pressed the paper to her eyes. "I have to fix myself up. Maybe if I apologize . . ."

"Apologize?" Hannah said sharply. "Apologize for what? For living?" Hannah looked at Deirdre's reflection in the mirror. She was applying makeup the Mary Plunkett way. "How could you do that?"

"Do what? Put on makeup?" Deirdre pulled down her sweater and tucked a few strands of hair behind her ear. "Just because you don't have a boyfriend, you want me to let Pete go." Deirdre wet a finger and dabbed at a black smudge under her eye.

"That's not true," Hannah said indignantly. "There are plenty of nice guys out there who will treat you better." She paused. "With respect." So what if it made her sound like a goody two-shoes.

"Oh, like George?" Deirdre laughed. "He was so nice to you, he made you sick." She took another piece of towel and blotted her fresh lipstick carefully on it.

"At least he didn't try to get me drunk," said Hannah. "Deirdre, I'm on your side."

"Right," said Deirdre, and she threw the paper towel into the toilet and flushed. Then she walked out the door and slammed it shut.

Hannah watched the paper towel swirl around and around in the water. It disappeared and then floated to the top. A pair of pink lips circled slowly in the bowl.

She reached down and gingerly lifted the paper out of the water, throwing it with a shudder into the wastebasket. Then she washed her hands and smoothed back her hair. Closing the toilet lid, she sat. It was peaceful in here, with the basket of pink shell soaps and the dish of pale rose petals. Even the buzz of the fluorescent lights soothed her. She knew she would have ditched Pete long before now. Why hadn't Deirdre? Maybe Pete was saving Deirdre from Mrs. Kiley. Maybe that's what Deirdre thought. People can't save you from unhappiness. Hannah knew that. She opened the door and entered the smoke-filled living room again.

Hannah searched the room for Steve, but there was no sign of him anywhere. It was too late to walk home, and too far anyway. She had money for a taxi—her mother made her hide an emergency ten-dollar bill in her wallet—but she'd feel stupid calling one.

Deirdre was talking to Pete again, and Hannah could hear her say "Please, please, Pete." She felt embarrassed for Deirdre, and hated the smug look on Pete's face. He crushed a beer can with one hand and tossed it into a nearby potted plant. Hannah watched as Deirdre stroked his arm. The look on Deirdre's face made her feel awful—it reminded Hannah of her mother the night before Grandpa's funeral. She was on the phone with her brother. Joseph, please come, her mother had pleaded with him. Mom will be so upset if you don't. He must have said no, because her mother said, Forget about the past and do it for me, then. She looked so desperate, and Hannah asked her father why Joseph wouldn't come. He looked distracted and said it was a long story. Then he walked away as Hannah's mother cried "Please," tears running down her face. Hannah couldn't look at her.

She didn't want to look at Deirdre either, but she couldn't take her eyes away. She was crying again, and at last Pete hooked an arm around Deirdre's neck, caressing her bare shoulder. He said something to her, and she hiccuped and laughed at the same time. Pete reached for another beer and took a swig, handing the rest of it to Deirdre. She sipped it and looked up to find Hannah watching. Pete saw her, too, and he whispered something to Deirdre.

Please don't come over, thought Hannah, but they were already walking toward her, Pete leaning heavily on Deirdre.

"We're leaving," he said. "Are you ready to go?"

"We'll drop you off at my house," Deirdre said urgently.

Hannah couldn't look at her. Pete was too drunk to drive. She'd sound like a fool saying it. She hesitated. "I'll see you at home. I'm going to stay a little while."

"What for?" said Pete. "You making it with someone, or what? I haven't noticed any heavy action." His eyes were bloodshot, and his nose and cheeks were very red. Deirdre stood and played with her beer can, popping the metal in and out.

"Frankly," said Hannah, "you're too drunk to drive." Relief flooded her. She knew she sounded like a television message, but she'd said it. "I value my life. And yours, Deirdre. Let's take a taxi."

"Frankly, schoolteacher," Pete said, "I don't give a damn." He took Deirdre's hand and pulled her. Deirdre stood her ground for a second and then let Pete lead her out the door.

Hannah was glad when they were gone, and vaguely wondered if Pete had ever seen *Gone With the Wind*, or had he actually thought up the line himself? He was no Rhett Butler. Maybe Steve was right—Deirdre deserved him. She walked into the kitchen and reached for the telephone. Steve was there, his head in the refrigerator. "What's up?" he said.

"I'm calling a cab to go home," said Hannah, embarrassed.

"It's only midnight. What's the matter, do you turn into a pumpkin or something?"

"You were right about Pete," said Hannah. "I wouldn't drive home with them, because he's drunk."

Steve shut the refrigerator door. "Nothing to eat in this house," he said. "Look, my brother is coming to get me soon. He'll give you a lift." He ripped open a bag of pretzel rods and bit into one. "Are they back together, then?"

"Who?" said Hannah, pouring herself some soda. "Oh, Pete and Deirdre. For the moment, I guess." She rinsed out her cup and placed it in the drainer. Steve wanted Deirdre, she didn't want him. Hannah wanted Richard, he didn't know what he wanted. What was it that awful T-shirt said?: Life's a bitch and then you die. Poor Grandpa. Poor Hannah. Poor Steve. Even poor Deirdre. Not poor Pete. "I don't know how she stays with him," she said to Steve.

"Like I said, some people have no taste." Steve looked at his watch. "He should be here soon."

"Maybe if she knew you really liked her, she'd ditch Pete." Hannah leaned against the refrigerator. It was cool against her back. Her feet hurt, and she felt hot and tired and unloved. Steve looked upset. She hated when her father looked upset. It unsettled her. She didn't even like Steve, but she heard herself trying to make him feel better. "I could say something to her . . ." Hannah's voice trailed off.

"Plenty of fish in the sea," said Steve. "Listen, Rich and I usually go to the movies on Friday nights. Why don't you and a friend come by? I'm tired of hearing Rich talk about you."

Hannah's feet stopped hurting. Richard had been talking about her. Hallelujah! "Okay," she said. "Maybe Deirdre will come." She willed her voice to sound like a shrug of the shoulders.

"Whatever," Steve shrugged back. His cheek twitched,

betrayed him, and he added, "Put in a good word for me."

The doorbell rang, and Steve looked at his watch again. "That's got to be my brother," he said. "Come on, Cinderella. It's after midnight."

16

Hannah had a jelly doughnut for breakfast. She ate slowly, savoring each tiny bite. She waited for the jelly prize. The clutter on the table no longer bothered her. She examined it, analyzed it with interest. Maybe Mrs. Kiley collected junk because it made her feel better. Safer. She took another bite, and the sweet taste of jelly hit her palate. Delicious. Like life. Jelly oozed onto her fingers, and she licked it off.

She heard a shuffling sound upstairs and hoped it was Deirdre. When Hannah had come in last night, she had no idea if Deirdre was back or not. The front door was unlocked, and she had slipped upstairs. There wasn't a sound in the house. Later she thought she heard the door open and close and the sound of a car roaring away.

Deirdre came into the kitchen and filled up the teakettle with water.

"I think I have a hangover," she said. "My dad sometimes drinks tea." She stood watching the kettle and added, "Not that he has that many hangovers."

Hannah considered eating a glazed doughnut, too, and wished she was like some people, who ate when they were depressed and stopped eating when they were happy. It was the other way around with Hannah.

"I'm sorry I didn't go home with you last night," she said, "but I was worried about Pete's driving." One jelly doughnut was enough.

"I'm sorry about last night, too," said Deirdre. "I get a little crazy where Pete is concerned."

Hannah tried to change the subject. Deirdre didn't like to hear criticism of Pete, and that was all she had to say. How do you tell your best friend her boyfriend is a jerk? "Steve Talbot has a crush on you," she said. "He asked us to go to the movies on Friday. Richard has been talking about me." She watched Deirdre's face to see if it registered interest. It didn't.

"Pete wants me to go all the way," Deirdre blurted out. "And I'm just not sure." She toyed with a piece of cruller, crushing it into little crumbs with her fork.

Hannah thought for a moment. Be careful, she told herself. "I was talking to my sister about it," she said. "You know, about knowing when you're ready. I mean, I knew I didn't ever want to do it with George."

"What did she say?"

"She said if a person is thinking about having sex, and she has to sit down and ask herself if she's ready, then she's not." Hannah took a knife and cut into a glazed doughnut. "So why don't you just wait?"

"I guess," said Deirdre. "But he's just so . . . insistent. He says if I loved him, I'd do it. I'd want to."

"If he loves you, he'll wait." She bit into the doughnut. "I love this stuff. I wish my mother was a junk-food addict."

"Fattening," said Deirdre. "You're full of advice today for a girl who's had two boyfriends that you hated."

"I'll ignore that." Hannah poked Deirdre. "I just hope I can follow my own advice." She wiped her mouth with a napkin. "One more piece of advice. I can't help it. If you do it, I hope you'll use birth control."

Deirdre looked at her, amazed. "Yes, Dr. Ruth. Are you going to buy me a pack of rubbers?"

"No, but I'll steal one from my father's drawer if you promise me you won't get pregnant."

"You know where he keeps them?"

"Sure. I'd get you my mother's diaphragm, but it wouldn't be hygienic."

Deirdre started to laugh. "I'm going to puke up my cruller!" she said. She looked serious again. "You'd do that for me? Steal a condom, I mean?"

"Sure," said Hannah. "He doesn't count them. Jean and I found one when we were little, and we thought it was a balloon. We even blew it up!"

Deirdre laughed loudly, her shoulders shaking and her earrings swinging wildly.

"What's so funny?" Hannah said, starting to laugh.

"I was just thinking. So long as it wasn't a used one!"

"Oh, gross! You are so disgusting!" cried Hannah, but she felt like they were friends again.

Hannah walked the long way to her house. It was only ten thirty, and her lesson was in half an hour. The sidewalk was icy, and the bare tree branches etched into a blue sky. She felt happier than she had in a long time. She felt like she was growing up. She was responsible for herself. She was right to break up with George, even if it meant she no longer had a boyfriend. She hadn't been bullied into taking drugs or having sex. And she had told Deirdre how she felt, a little. Hannah rounded the corner, and the old watermill came into view. Some children were playing by the ice, and she thought she could see patches of water on it. She conjured up the vision of a drowning child, hands flailing at the jagged ice, ice breaking. A man went over to the children and shook his finger at them. She laughed as he dragged them away kicking and screaming. Saved. For a split second she saw Grandma leaping forward, and she shook the image away. She would call her tonight.

Hannah took out her house key and opened the door. It was good to be home again—a wall of books, her mother's teakwood furniture, the moss-green couch that her mother picked because her father liked the outdoors, and pots of African violets everywhere.

She took her violin out of the closet and set up the music stand. Tuning the violin, she caressed its smooth surface with her chamois cloth. She practiced a little. The sunlight was filtering through her mother's new wooden blinds. The music took over, and she played with feeling—a perfect melding of control and emotion. She had a smile on her face when the doorbell rang.

Mr. Kreutzer arrived, dapper and cheerful, and she hung up his overcoat, the familiar scent of his cologne in her nostrils. Stench, her father called it. She played her Bach piece for him and did some scales, and he looked pleased. Then he casually asked Hannah where her parents were. She told him, and then he played a difficult section of Prokofiev's *Love for Three Oranges* with her. She didn't want to mess up at orchestra rehearsal.

"I have a surprise for you," Mr. Kreutzer said, and he pulled out a crisp new sheet of music—a duet for two violins. Hannah played it alone at first. "Sight-reading's good practice for you," he told her. Then they played together slowly, until she was more familiar with the music. Finally they played it faster, swaying in time to the music. It was a lilting piece, and Mr. Kreutzer made little yelping sounds as his fingers scurried across the strings. Hannah wondered if it ever bothered the other orchestra members, his noisy playing. Or did he yelp only during private lessons? Did he know he did it?

"It's past our hour," said Mr. Kreutzer, checking his watch.

"Oh, one more time!" cried Hannah, and she played it all the way through with confidence.

"I really must go now," he said, and he put away his violin and stood by the closet waiting for Hannah to hand him his coat. First he arranged his scarf, smoothing it across his chest, and then his overcoat, reeking of perfume.

"Well, dear girl," he said, "I must go." Hannah hugged him good-bye. Trembling, he pulled her against him so hard that his glasses hit her forehead. The cologne was overwhelming and she felt like gagging. She pulled away weakly, not wanting to insult him. He gripped her tightly and pulled her to him again. She felt his mouth against her forehead, open and wet, and then his hands cupped hard around her face, fingers gripping her cheeks as he pushed his lips against hers. She felt his tongue in her mouth. Someone was screaming—was it her?—and she pushed herself away, hard. Her stomach was heaving. Her face was wet. She ran upstairs into the bathroom, locking the door behind her. She sat on the toilet seat, hunched over her knees, and listened for the click of the front door closing. At last she heard it, and the sound of a car motor, too.

She sat staring at the bathtub, so round and white, with traces of fishes and seahorses on it, old stickers that she had pasted there. All faded now. She turned on the hot water full force.

Hannah stood and faced the medicine cabinet. She reached for her toothbrush, the red one, and applied a strip of toothpaste. She put it into her mouth, brushed vigorously around her molars, her eyeteeth. Panic seized her and she threw the brush into the sink. Was it her toothbrush? Or was it her father's? She ran the brush under hot tap water, rubbed the bristles guiltily on the hand towel, and placed it back in its slot. Opening the medicine cabinet, she took out a brown bottle of hydrogen peroxide, so good for canker sores, and poured some directly into her mouth. She swigged it, like Deirdre drinking beer. Gagging, she spat it into the sink.

Hannah lay in the bath with her feet stretched out so that they could touch the chrome faucet. She turned on more hot water with her toes. Her breasts were barely covered, and she soaked a washcloth in the hot water and draped it over the two small bumps. She remembered when she and her sister were little and Jean had stood up in the bathtub and peed straight into Hannah's mouth. She screamed, so long and so loudly that her mother burst into the bathroom looking terrified. Hannah stood up in the water and said, "She peed in my mouth and it was salty," and started to laugh. Her mother laughed so hard she sat right down on the bath mat. The image faded. Mr. Kreutzer's tongue was in her mouth again. She pulled her knees up to her chest, fetal-like, but she felt unprotected. A naked body in a porcelain coffin.

She scrambled out of the bathtub and dried herself methodically with a fresh towel. Starting at her feet, she rubbed hard, and traveled upward to her belly, her breasts, her neck, her face. She imagined bits of skin flying into the air. Her mother's towels were always pink, and she thought idly that they should be brownish or grayish or even black. She unlocked the door. Her thoughts kept jumping back to the kiss, if that was what it was called, and she caught a glimpse of her face in the mirror, twisted and strange. In her bedroom she put on clean clothes without checking to see if anything matched.

It was the same sunlit day outside, but it felt colder. A bicycle lay abandoned on its side on the frozen dirt lawn next door, red curtains in the windows and a fresh green wreath with a red bow on the door. Mrs. Kolinsky always decorated seasonally, her slipcovers and curtains autumnal colors in the fall, light pastels in the spring, and pale blues in the summertime to make the house appear cooler. Today it was all Christmas cheer. Hannah wanted to rip the wreath down.

She crossed the street, preferring to pass Mrs. Dickert's house, plain white, no decorations, quite puritan. Then a row of drab houses as she headed toward town, with porches full of nosy people in the summertime. Thank goodness it was winter. No one could ask her how her parents were doing, how school was. Shove it, she would tell them. She passed the same old stores with their tired Christmas decorations, the old luncheonette with its silly sign in the window: HELP WANTED. GRUMPY PEOPLE NEED NOT APPLY. They probably didn't pay enough. The ceramics shop full of ugly statuettes of kittens and Little Bo Peeps who lost their sheep. A bomb through the window would be nice. Finally, at the corner, the drugstore where Deirdre bought Pete a million cards full of "I love you" and "I miss you" and "You make my life complete." Pictures of adorable pigs, fluffy teddy bears, heart-shaped boxes full of candy—all extolling Pete. It made her want to vomit.

Past the movie theater, divided into four small auditoriums now. The huge decorated ceiling was gone, and the plush purple velvet curtains with the huge gold tassels, too. Rowen's, with its ugly nightgowns hanging in the window. The whole town looked ugly.

Hannah crossed a small bridge that spanned the river and sat on a bench, pulling her coat around her and fishing her mittens and beret out of her pocket. This was the park where the Girl Scouts met and marched in the Memorial Day parade. It seemed so long ago, before boys and clothes and where to go to college were ever important. Tears filled her eyes and rolled down her cheeks. She didn't bother to brush them away.

A bicycle whizzed past, and she heard the jingle of a bell, but she didn't look up. Then Bobby Mack sat down beside her.

"Are you okay?"

Hannah quickly brushed away her tears. "I'm in a bad mood," she said.

"How come?" he said, blowing on his hands and rubbing them together.

"I just am." She wished he would go away.

"Is there anything I can do?" He didn't move.

Hannah felt the tears well up again and said, "Don't be so nice to me."

"Did something happen? Is it your grandfather, or is someone else sick?"

Hannah saw the concern in his eyes. She plucked at the

red cap sticking out of his pocket and said, "You'd better put this on before you freeze to death."

"I can't," said Bobby, smiling.

"Why not? It's practically below zero out."

"It'll flatten my hair," said Bobby. "I look terrible with a flattop."

"And they say women are vain?" Hannah pulled the cap out of Bobby's pocket and put it on his head. "There. You look very fetching."

"All right. For you, I'll keep it on. But just for that, you're going ice-skating with me. I always ice-skate if I'm wearing my flattop hat." Bobby looked questioningly at her. "What do you say?"

"My ankles are too weak," Hannah said. "And I don't own any skates."

"So wear my sister's. And my ankles are strong," he said, "like tree trunks." Bobby jumped up and took the position of Mr. Universe, flexing his muscles this way and that. He rolled up his pant leg and extended his ankle. "Look. Me He-man. You Weak-ankle Woman. Me teach."

Hannah couldn't help laughing. "Okay, okay," she said. "But I'm warning you. I'm a real klutz."

"I only skate with klutzes," Bobby said. He took her arm and pulled her off the bench. "We'll take my bike back to the house and grab the skates."

"Promise me one thing, Bobby," said Hannah.

"What's that?"

"Roll down your pant leg first."

"And I thought you loved me for my ankles!" he sobbed. "Remember, klutz. The best thing about ice-skating is the hot chocolate afterward."

"Good," said Hannah. "I'm a very talented drinker." It

sounded delicious. She would erase the morning from her memory. It never happened.

Bobby bent over Hannah and laced her ice skates, threading each hole and pulling the laces tightly as he went. The tip of his tongue stuck out of the corner of his mouth as if this were serious business. He finished one skate and turned solemnly to the other. Hannah looked down at his red-capped head almost tenderly.

"Ready?" said Bobby. His knees cracked when he stood up. "I knew that would happen. I try to be gallant and my knees crack."

"It's your ankles I care about, not your knees." Hannah stood up, wobbled, and braced herself against Bobby. Taking her hand away, she inched toward the frozen river, holding on to tree branches and bushes until she reached the ice. She placed one foot on the surface.

"Are you sure this ice will hold me?" She remembered the children playing on the ice by the old watermill. An omen? No, the morning didn't exist. She placed the other foot on the surface, took a sliding step, and felt her feet wobble and slip out from under her. She sat right down on her bottom.

"Where's the railing?" she wailed. "I need a railing!"

"Courage," said Bobby, and he skated onto the ice, etching a figure eight in front of her and stopping expertly. "Let me help you up," he said, extending his hand. Hannah took it and fell back again with such force that she took Bobby with her.

"You'd think it wouldn't hurt," she said, rubbing her backside, "with my padded rear end."

Bobby pulled her up again, and this time she managed

to stay standing. "Turn around," he said, and he started brushing bits of snow off her jacket. His hand stopped in midair as he reached her backside. "You'd better do that yourself," he said, drawing back quickly. "As much as I'd like to." Hannah couldn't tell if he was blushing or if it was the winter air, because he turned his face away.

After a few more spills, they managed to skate together arm in arm. Hannah began to enjoy it, though she felt a little like a sidecar on a motorcycle. Bobby started singing and told her it was obvious she was a musician because she appreciated good music.

"Appreciate it?" said Hannah. "I'm skating in time to it. You're singing a Strauss waltz, Bobby, and I'm very impressed."

"And I didn't even know it. You'll have to educate me," he said, "because I just call that my ice-skating song."

They skated toward the bank again and Bobby said, "Time for hot chocolate."

They sat down and unlaced their skates. Hannah felt just as wobbly with her skates off, and she took Bobby's arm again. She felt comfortable doing it, and when Bobby started singing "We're off to see the wizard, the wonderful wizard of Oz," she joined in and nearly drowned him out.

A wave of warmth hit them as they entered the luncheonette. Waitresses bustled back and forth, plates were clinking, people were eating and talking. Hannah felt like she was back in the real world. With Bobby Mack, of all people. Deirdre would never believe it. But sitting opposite him in a red vinyl booth, the frivolity of skating on a frozen river was beginning to fade. Hannah clasped her hands together and gazed down at them.

"Have you thawed out yet?" Bobby asked, handing her a menu.

Hannah took it gratefully. She could stare at the menu and not at her hands or, even worse, at Bobby.

"Almost," said Hannah. "I had a junk-food breakfast, so I'd better have some real food."

"An omelet?" suggested Bobby. "That's what I'm having."

"Sounds good," said Hannah as the waitress appeared. "A cheese omelet, no hash browns, please."

"I'll eat her hash browns," said Bobby. "Make that two omelets with whole wheat toast. And two hot chocolates, please. Keeping you healthy, Hannah." Bobby handed the waitress the menus and knocked over the saltshaker.

"Feh, feh," he spat, and threw some salt over his left shoulder. "I'm warding off evil spirits, and in the meantime I've given the man behind me a good case of dandruff."

Hannah smiled weakly. The memory of Mr. Kreutzer, trembling and panting, filled her head, buzzed inside her. She started shredding the corner of her placemat.

"What is it, Hannah? I shouldn't have ordered whole wheat toast for you? You're mad at me? What?"

"Sorry. I'm just a drag. My mind is wandering." The placemat was now a pile of shredded paper.

"Why sorry? Tell me what's the matter." Bobby leaned forward, and his breath scattered the pile. "You look so sad. You've got the same woe-is-me look you had this morning. I thought I'd taken you away from all that."

"You did," said Hannah. "I forgot all about it while we were skating." She traced a line through the scattered paper.

"Forgot about what?"

Hannah leaned on her elbow and covered her mouth with her hand. If she told him, it would all be real again. She took her hand away. "I had my music lesson this morning. At my house. My parents are away," Hannah said. There. It was out. She avoided looking at Bobby's face. "And my teacher—" She stopped.

"What? Your teacher what?" Bobby touched her hand. "Died? Had a heart attack? What?"

"He stuck his tongue in my mouth." She'd said it. Now Bobby could think whatever he wanted.

Bobby sat dumbstruck. For once he didn't say a word.

The waitress arrived with their omelets and hot chocolate. Hannah held her hot chocolate and lifted it to her face. The steam warmed her as she sipped the sweet liquid.

Bobby spoke. "He attacked you." His voice was very low.

"I don't know if you could call it an attack. I've known him for eight years. We sometimes hug good-bye after my lesson." Hannah felt like crying again. "What am I going to do? I feel so confused."

"You're going to tell your parents," said Bobby. "As soon as they come home you're going to tell them. And stop taking lessons from the creep."

"I can't do it," groaned Hannah, "I just can't." She poked her omelet with her fork. It was cold now, and the orange cheese had hardened around the edges. "What if they don't believe me?"

"Why wouldn't they? I've read about this stuff, Hannah. You feel guilty even though you haven't done anything!" Bobby banged his hand on the table, and the waitress scurried over. "Nothing, thanks. I'm just making a point to my friend here," he said.

"But maybe I was too friendly . . . I don't know." Hannah covered her eyes.

"Hannah." Bobby waited until she looked at him. "He's a dirty old man."

"He is, isn't he?" Hannah said in a small voice.

"So you'll tell them tomorrow," Bobby said firmly.

"Couldn't I just quit playing the violin?"

"Is that what you want to do?"

"Not really." Hannah's stomach growled. The omelet was congealed rubber, the hot chocolate was cold.

"Do you want to see that dirty old man teacher of yours again?"

Hannah shook her head violently and said, "No way!"

"Then what do you have to do?"

"Tell my parents."

"Right. I feel like I'm coaching a football team or something."

"Rah, rah, rah." Hannah cheered with a limp hand. "Bobby?"

"What?" Bobby sighed loudly, wiping imaginary sweat off his brow.

"I'm starving."

"So we'll split a tuna fish sandwich." He signaled to the waitress. "Okay?"

"Okay." Hannah gave the waitress their order and added, "On whole wheat bread, please."

It snowed heavily that night, and Hannah and Deirdre stayed home to trim the Christmas tree. Under his wife's direction, Mr. Kiley had struggled to set up the tree that afternoon, and it had moved from one corner of the living room to the other before settling by the stairway.

Every ornament was carefully wrapped in tissue paper, and Hannah was afraid she would break one as Mrs. Kiley's watchful eyes bored into her.

"Hey, my snowman!" Deirdre tore the tissue paper away from three misshapen balls of hardened clay, the snowman's face all crooked smile. "Isn't he cute? I made him in kindergarten, didn't I, Dad?"

"Donna made it," said Mrs. Kiley. "The head fell off yours last year."

"Let me see it, Dee," said Mr. Kiley, holding out his hand. "It has the initials D.K. on the back, Ethel. So it could be either one of them." He handed it back to Deirdre.

"I tell you the head broke off Deirdre's snowman," said Mrs. Kiley, her voice rising. "What is it, Herb? Do you always have to contradict me? In front of your daughter and in front of her friend? I say black and you say white. Anyone can see that this one is Donna's. It's neater."

"Ethel, I'm only saying this might be—"

"You hate to admit you're wrong," she cut in. Mrs. Kiley turned to Hannah. "I say black, he says white."

Hannah hung a red ball on a low branch of the tree and tried to avoid looking at Deirdre's mother. She's like a bull in one of those cartoons, Hannah thought. Steam will start coming from her nose any minute.

Mrs. Kiley wanted sympathy. She took hold of Hannah's sleeve and said, "It's like that old song. You probably don't know it—Fred Astaire says, 'You say tomato and I say tomahto,' you know, they pronounce it different ways. That's life with him." She gestured toward her husband. " 'Tomato, tomahto, potato, potahto, let's call the whole thing off' . . . except he sings it to Ginger Rogers. What's the matter, Herb, aren't I Ginger Rogersy enough for you?" She sneered.

Mr. Kiley whirled around and grabbed his wife by the shoulders. "You want to know what's the matter? You want contradicting? Huh, Ethel?" He smiled at her, but it was an ugly smile. "Say hello. Tell me hello," he said.

"No," said Mrs. Kiley, tight-lipped.

"Tell me hello!" he shouted, his fingers tightening their grip.

"Hello! What do you want from my life?" Mrs. Kiley cried.

"Good-bye!" he shouted. "Good-bye, that's what I want. You say hello and I say good-bye and good riddance!" And he walked out the door.

"Don't you walk out on me!" cried Mrs. Kiley, running after him.

Hannah busied herself unwrapping a tiny Santa and handed it to Deirdre. Deirdre hooked it on the tree and picked up the abandoned snowman. "Little man," she said, "let's put you way up high where you'll be protected." She climbed up the stairs and hooked him close to the top of the tree.

"He's pretty," said Hannah softly.

"He is, isn't he?" said Deirdre. She stepped back to admire him. "Donna probably made him. Mother always knows best, you know." She bent and picked up a silver star, rubbing it against her sweater.

"You could have made him," said Hannah. "You've always been good at art. Don't put yourself down like that."

"You have this warped idea that I've got it all together, don't you? Boys and clothes and school. Well, I don't."

Hannah shrugged. "Nobody's perfect," she said.

Deirdre turned and looked sharply at Hannah. Hannah started to smile. Deirdre tried to hold on to her fierceness, and the silver star trembled in her hand.

"Do you know who I'd like to hang on that tree?" Deirdre said.

"Your mother!" Hannah said loudly, and she clapped a hand over her mouth. Deirdre snorted, and the noise turned into laughter as she climbed the stairs again and leaned over the banister.

"There," said Deirdre, a wide smile on her face as she placed the star on top of the tree. "Merry Christmas."

17

*H*annah's parents came home on Sunday afternoon.

"It's good to be back," her mother said with a sigh, hanging her coat in the closet. "Hello, pretty plants, I missed you." She went straight to the watering can and started watering them.

Her father surveyed the house. "It doesn't look like you had any wild parties here, Hannah," he joked. "We missed you, but you would have been bored—or overworked. All we did was pack and clean and eat, and then we started all over again. Your mother and I are exhausted. Aren't we, Phyllis?"

Hannah's mother looked distracted, and some of the water spilled onto the teak coffee table. "Hannah, could you get me a dry cloth?"

Hannah handed her a paper towel. "How's Grandma?"

"She's upset," said her father. "It's to be expected. We had to pack up all of Julius's suits for the Goodwill people, and then we had to throw out all of his shoes."

"Couldn't you have given them away to someone in the

building?" said Hannah. A garbage can full of Grandpa's shoes. She didn't want to think about it.

Her father's voice was gentle. "It's a Jewish tradition not to give away used shoes. No one else is supposed to walk in your shoes after you've died."

"They were all polished and in a line," said her mother. "Grandma cried like a baby." She turned to Hannah, her voice strained. "So what did you do this weekend?"

"Deirdre and I went to a party on Friday," said Hannah. Don't ask how it was.

"And how was it?"

"It was okay."

"And Saturday?" Mrs. Gold sprayed some furniture polish on the table and wiped it dry. "I hope the water doesn't stain this wood," she mumbled to herself.

"I went ice-skating, and then we trimmed the tree in the evening." Hannah looked quickly at her mother's face to see if she'd noticed skipping the Saturday morning's music lesson. She hadn't. The plants were taking all of her attention.

Mrs. Gold plucked out a dry leaf. "I didn't know you liked to ice-skate. And the Kileys? How are they?"

"I don't want to stay there again." Hannah opened the window a crack. "It's stuffy in here, isn't it?"

"I hadn't noticed." Mrs. Gold ran the paper towel over the leaves of a rubber plant. "Why don't you want to stay there again?"

"Because they fight all the time, and Deirdre is a mess. She's so cute and funny, and she gets crazy with her mother, and she runs to her boyfriend like he's . . . I don't know."

"What? Like he's a god?" her mother said sharply. "They

treat their sons like princes and then the sons go off and leave them. The daughters clean up all the messes."

"Harvey is nice to his parents, Mom. And Donna lives out of state. Mrs. Kiley just doesn't seem to be able to get along with Deirdre."

Mr. Gold arrived with a tray of tea. "I'm not sure that your mother is talking about Deirdre's brother." He handed his wife a cup and put a plate of oatmeal cookies on the coffee table.

Mrs. Gold took the teacup, and some of the tea spilled into the saucer. "I'm spilling everything today!" She sighed and placed a napkin underneath the cup. "God knows I love my brother. But he can't even come to his own father's funeral, and who calls him up and tells him she loves him? Grandma. Like nothing has happened." Mrs. Gold took a sip of tea. "So Deirdre runs to her boyfriend?"

"Not so much like a god," said Hannah. "Like he's saving her life or something."

"Maybe he is," said her father. "It's a shame, but maybe he is."

"But he treats her just like her parents do." Hannah tried to resist the oatmeal cookies. She broke one in half and ate it. "They treat her like shit." She waited for a reprimand from her mother but none came. "They tear each other apart, and then they take it out on her." She ate the lonely other cookie half.

"If you hadn't eaten it, I would have. How do they treat her like shit?" asked her mother, a small smile on her lips.

"I'm serious! They tear each other apart at breakfast, lunch, and dinner. Yesterday it looked as if Mr. Kiley was going to hit her," said Hannah. "It was horrible."

"Hit who? Deirdre?" said Mr. Gold, concern in his voice.

"No, his wife," said Hannah.

"Maybe we should have taken you with us," said her mother. "I just didn't think you'd be very happy."

"Mom," said Hannah, "I survived. I'm just saying they don't have a marriage like you and Daddy do. You know . . ." Her voice wavered. "Mutual respect and all that—"

"Stuff?" her father interrupted. "I let it go the first time." He glanced at his wife. "Everybody has problems."

"We fight too," said Mrs. Gold, looking back. "You just don't hear us. We're not the perfect couple, you know." She smoothed Hannah's hair away from her face and said almost apologetically, "I wish we were."

Mr. Gold suddenly stood up. "I'd better go shovel some snow before someone slips on the sidewalk and gives me a lawsuit for Christmas."

"Hanukkah," said Hannah. "I'll help." Ever since Hannah was little and their neighbor had dropped dead shoveling his sidewalk, Hannah took it upon herself to help her father clear the snow. The ambulance had arrived, its sirens screaming and lights flashing, and she saw Mr. Fletcher, arm dangling from a stretcher and Mrs. Fletcher sobbing beside him. Hannah got hysterical when her father went out later to clear his own driveway and to finish clearing poor Mr. Fletcher's. "Don't go, Daddy!" she cried, and her father coaxed her into helping him. "If you help me, I won't work too hard."

They put on their old jackets and heavy boots, and Mr. Gold handed Hannah the lighter shovel. He was faster than she was, and he cleared his half of the driveway and most of the sidewalk before Hannah could finish. They worked in silence, except for the crunching of the snow and an occasional grunt as a heavy load was lifted. At last they finished, and her father took both shovels and jammed them into the fresh pile of snow.

"Hot chocolate!" he said. "How about a walk into town?"

Hannah nodded, and they started walking, stomping through some of the unshoveled walks, sliding across frozen patches, and crunching on salt as they reached the stores.

It felt strange to Hannah to be sitting in the same luncheonette, sipping hot chocolate with cold hands. Mr. Gold munched on some cinnamon toast and cleared his throat.

"Your mother has decided to go to Arizona for the Christmas break," he said.

"Arizona!" said Hannah. "Christmas is ten days away. Can we get tickets?"

"Not us," said her father. "Just your mother."

"Why would she want to go without us? I have two weeks off from school!" Hannah protested.

"Who knows what's going on in her mind," said her father glumly. "Since your grandpa's death, she hasn't been herself. She feels she needs"—he waved his hand through the air—"time to herself."

"Time for what?"

"Hannah. Her father just died. Her only brother didn't come. She wants to see him," her father said flatly. "I just can't tell you any more, because I don't know any more. Your mother says family is important to her, especially now, and Joe is family."

"She'd rather be with him than us? He didn't even come to his own father's funeral!" Hannah said fiercely.

Mr. Gold pushed his empty cup away from him and leaned an elbow on the table. "There's more to it than that," he said. "Joe thought he had his reasons."

"What kind of person wouldn't come to his own father's funeral?" Hannah's face was flushed. "Nothing would stop me from coming to your—" She stopped abruptly.

"I'm so glad, honey," her father said dryly. "Listen. Years ago your uncle met a girl named Rose, and he started taking her out. Finally he took her home to meet his parents, and they were very nice to her. You know, Grandma and Grandpa are very hospitable people. Grandpa would give you the shirt off his back."

"And what happened? Uncle Joe married Aunt Rose, didn't he?"

"He did. But Rose wasn't Jewish, and Grandpa sat *shivah* for Uncle Joe, his own son. Grandma begged him not to, but he was like a crazy man."

"Why would Grandpa go into mourning for his son? That *is* crazy," said Hannah.

"Because if you marry outside the religion, you're considered by some to be dead. So Grandpa declared his son Joe dead. Grandma had to sneak out of the house to see them. They were married by then, with a baby. Your cousin Mark."

"Grandpa did that? Sweet old Grandpa? He couldn't." Hannah sat back in disbelief.

"He did. Later there was a reconciliation, but relations were still stiff. And then when Rose divorced Joe, Grandpa said if he'd listened to him and married a Jewish girl, none of this would have happened."

"I can't believe it. Sweet old Grandpa," Hannah repeated, stunned.

"I'm sure it's easier being a grandfather than a father," said Mr. Gold. "Grandpa added insult to injury and told Joe that the family was disgraced by a divorce. And Joe never spoke to him again."

"How awful!" Hannah said indignantly. "It's worse than the Kileys! At least they talk to each other. Why didn't anyone ever tell me about this?"

Her father shrugged. "It was a family tragedy. I guess we felt you weren't old enough." He shifted in his seat. "Look, Hannah." He had on his end-of-the—lecture face. "Grandma forgives him. Your mother is trying to forgive him. She's going to see him, isn't she?" Mr. Gold fished in his pants pocket for his wallet. "And she needs her damned space," he muttered, counting out some bills. "So why don't we try and forgive him, and forgive your mother for leaving us, okay?" He dropped a five-dollar bill on the table. "Your mother would tell me I left too big a tip, you know. Let's get going." He slipped on his jacket and scarf, and without turning to see if Hannah was following, walked out the door.

By then it was too late to tell him about the music lesson.

"I heard about the wild party, Hannah." Richard arched his arm across her like a bridge as she rotated the dial on her combination lock. Her heart did its usual dance. The combination went right out of her head.

She did quick inventory and cursed herself for throwing on a pale yellow sweater that accentuated her small chest and washed out her face.

"It was wild, all right," she said.

"Up to your old tricks again, huh?"

"Wouldn't you like to know?" She shrouded her face in mystery. At least she hoped it was mystery and not craziness.

"Wait for me, would you?" said Richard. "I'm just going to get my books."

Bobby's arm made a bridge above her and Hannah's heart did another turn . . . a guilty one. He spoke softly into her ear. "So what happened?" he said. "Did you tell them?"

She fiddled with her combination again. "I didn't get a chance," she said quickly. "My mother's a mess about my grandfather, and now she's going to Arizona, and my father's upset." She looked nervously down the hall toward Richard's locker. "I just couldn't," she said fiercely as she watched Richard slam the locker door.

Bobby stood there, silent.

"Damn it, Bobby, get off my case. It wasn't a very good weekend, and now I can't even remember my combination, you've got me so worked up."

"A good weekend?" Bobby said angrily. He lowered his voice to a whisper. "What happens next Saturday? Are you going to have a music lesson with him or what? A make-out session?"

Hannah couldn't look at him. She faced the locker and said coldly, "I'm sorry I ever told you about it." Her voice was controlled fury. "Just leave me alone, will you?"

"Hannah, I'm sorry." Bobby took her arm. "I didn't mean it. I said something stupid, okay?"

Hannah shook his arm away. "Richard?" she said loudly as he approached her locker.

"You rang?" He stepped toward her. "Your wish is my command," he said with a sweep of his hand.

"Can I borrow your English book?" Her heart was hammering. She could feel Bobby's presence, she could hear him breathing.

"Sure." Richard leaned over conspiratorially as they walked away. "So are we going to the movies on Friday?"

She felt tiny pangs as Bobby, walking behind them, stopped dead in his tracks. "As long as it's not a horror film," she said. She marveled at her newfound acting skills. She sounded downright lighthearted. She wanted to sing out to Bobby, "I'm sorry, forgive me." She wanted to tell him that it was all too painful to remember. She turned her head slightly to look for him, but he was gone.

After that, there was no doubt in Hannah's mind. Bobby avoided her. She never saw him in the hallway, and in English he arrived just as the bell rang. He sat staring straight ahead and never tapped her on the shoulder or made funny comments. He didn't mention the music lesson again. And it was as if their afternoon of ice-skating had never happened. To her surprise, she missed him.

18

By Thursday, Hannah was beginning to get butterflies in her stomach about meeting Richard. Deirdre and Pete had quarreled again, so Deirdre agreed half-heartedly to go.

Hannah spoke to Deirdre on the telephone. "It's a comedy, the one with Eddie Murphy. Do I look good when I laugh?"

"Adorable. How do we get there?" Deirdre said dully. "I'm not walking in the freezing cold."

"Deirdre, don't do me any favors," said Hannah, annoyed. "You've been dragging your feet about this whole thing. Do you want to go or not?"

"I guess. It just feels strange to be making plans without Pete. It makes me nervous."

"You're nervous? I'm meeting the guy I've had a crush on all year!" Hannah cupped her hand over the receiver and said to her mother, "Mom, if it's cold out tomorrow, can you or Dad give us a lift to the movies?"

Mrs. Gold arranged four slices of pizza on a pan and put it in the oven. "I guess so," she said. "Help me with the salad, will you?"

"My mother will drive us," said Hannah. She paused. "Are you sure I look adorable when I laugh?" She hung up without waiting for an answer.

Hannah took the wooden chopping board her mother handed her. "When's Dad coming home? He's late."

"Your father is at a cocktail party." She gave Hannah a peeler and some carrots.

"And you didn't go?" Hannah scraped the carrot peel into the garbage. "How come?"

"I just didn't feel like it," her mother said tersely. "Peel the cucumber, okay?" Mrs. Gold washed a few leaves of lettuce and shredded them into a bowl. "I need some time to myself, and to tell you the truth, I don't feel like making small talk at a stupid party."

"It might have taken your mind off . . . things. Shouldn't I keep the skin on? That's where all the nutrition is." Hannah waited for her mother to answer, peeler poised over the cucumber.

"If you want bitter cucumber," said her mother, "leave it on."

"I'll peel it," said Hannah, and she scraped off the of-fending green. "What's the matter between you and Dad?"

Mrs. Gold held out a scallion and looked at Hannah. "Onion?" she said.

"Not for me," said Hannah. "I can't afford bad breath."

Her mother put down the knife and sat next to Hannah. "You know I'm depressed," she said. "Since Grandpa." She took a deep breath and expelled the air slowly. "I just don't feel like doing anything." Her eyes darted to Hannah's face. "Not eating, or working, or . . . anything." She sighed again. "Your father feels neglected, and I—" A sob erupted from her, and she covered her mouth.

127

"What, Mom?" said Hannah, putting her arms around her mother. "What?"

"I feel bereft," she said.

Hannah didn't know what to say. She was so used to telling her mother her problems. Why did it make her feel so strange to hear her mother talk this way?

"Is that why you're going to Arizona? To be with Uncle Joe?"

Mrs. Gold brushed the tears away and said, "Partly. I feel like I'm treading water here. Like life is going on around me but I'm not a participant." She took out a tissue and blew her nose. "I feel empty," she said.

Hannah knew exactly what her mother meant. "Sometimes I feel like that—like when Deirdre got a boyfriend and I felt out of it. You told me it was just a phase I was going through."

Her mother smiled. "I guess I'm going through a phase, too," she said. "Just because you become an adult doesn't mean your problems suddenly disappear. Hopefully you'll be better equipped to deal with them."

It occurred to Hannah that her mother didn't seem any better equipped to deal with problems. Dead eyes, black rings under them. She resented it. She wanted her mother to be cheerful again, buoyant, like the framed fruits in her yellow kitchen. She wanted adulthood to mean the end of uncertainty and torture. Her mother's pained expression made her turn away. "When's supper?" she asked, throwing the chopped cucumber into the salad bowl.

"Right now," said her mother. She opened up the oven and shoveled a piece of pizza onto a plate. "Eat, honey," she said, handing it to her daughter.

Hannah squeezed her eyes half shut, kept the tears away.

She cut herself a mouthful and blew on it. "How about watching some TV with me later?" Her mother shook her head.

Hannah desperately wanted her mother to bounce back, to deliver one of those cheery maxims that drove her crazy. Hannah tried one herself. "Time heals," she said.

"I suppose," said her mother. "If you say so."

Hannah scattered half a dozen purple eyeliners across the bed. "Choose one," she said to Deirdre. "I have to dazzle Richard tonight."

Deirdre flipped a pencil over. "Misty Mauve. Sounds like someone's crying." She flipped another. "Purple Passion. Do you anticipate passion?"

"Don't get smart with me. I'll try it anyway." Hannah's hand shook as she drew a line across her lower lid. "Thank God for Q-tips. I'm a wreck." She held out her crammed makeup bag to Deirdre. "Do you want to borrow any-thing?"

"Who's there to impress?" said Deirdre, pushing back a strand of lank, unwashed hair. "I'm letting my natural beauty shine through."

"Since when do you go without makeup?" said Hannah, annoyed. "Do you only get dressed up for Pete? How about yourself?"

"You've been reading too many of those psychology books," said Deirdre. "Either that, or your mother is preaching again." She took out a pot of Vaseline and dabbed some on her lips. "Don't worry, I won't embarrass you. Besides," she said, running a comb through her hair, "maybe Pete will show up."

"He knows where you'll be?" said Hannah, horrified.

"I mentioned it to him, but we were fighting, so I don't know if he heard."

Wonderful, thought Hannah. Pete will come wandering through the movie house calling her name like Marlon Brando did in *A Streetcar Named Desire*. "We'd better get going," she said aloud. "We're walking."

"How come?" said Deirdre. "It's freezing out there!"

Hannah checked the back of herself in the mirror. Her rear end was no smaller than it had been a half an hour before. "My dad's not home yet and I can't ask my mother to drive us. She's . . . under the weather."

"It's the weather we're talking about," said Deirdre, putting on her coat. "Come on, then." She wound her scarf around her neck. "Let's go brave the elements."

There was a large crowd at the movie theater, and they stood at the end of the ticket buyers' line. Deirdre squinted as she searched through the milling people.

"Do you see them?" whispered Hannah.

"I'm looking for Pete," said Deirdre. She added hastily, "And don't look at me that way. I'll be very sweet and charming with Steve, if that's what you're worried about."

"He'd treat you a lot better than Pete does," said Hannah. She handed the girl behind the glass window a five-dollar bill, then took her ticket. "Let's go in. I'm freezing to death."

They entered the lobby. Ordinarily Hannah would pore over the mural of movie stars, identify them, criticize them. The Marilyn Monroe was too pasty, the Bette Midler looked like a clown . . . She ignored them, and the candy counter, too.

"No popcorn?" whispered Deirdre. "I'm amazed!"

"It would stick to my lip gloss," said Hannah. "Besides, my stomach is churning."

Steve and Richard were waving at them as they walked down the aisle. Deirdre went first, excusing herself as she stepped over people who were already seated. Richard removed his jacket from the seats he'd been saving, and she sat down. Hannah froze. How could Deirdre sit next to Richard? He stood up and said, "Let's make a switch here," and practically hauled Deirdre out of the seat and into the one next to Steve.

"Your cheeks are all red," he said as she settled her jacket behind her.

"It's cold out there," she said, wondering if her blush was too heavy. She'd have to go to the bathroom later to check.

Richard slid down in his seat and rested his feet on the empty seat in front of him. "They build these theaters for midgets," he said. Hannah slid down next to him and rested her feet next to his. "My father has the same problem," she said, and wanted to bite her tongue. It was definitely not cool to talk about your father. She searched her mind for something to say, something cute.

"How's your dog?" she asked, and she could have slit her throat.

"Fine!" He laughed. "Where did that come from?" He nudged her sneaker with his boot. "You've been out in the cold too long." He forgave her. Thank you, Lord, she breathed.

The lights dimmed, and Hannah sat up in her seat. She always felt a thrill when a movie started, and she hoped Richard wasn't the type to talk. The credits came on, and Richard said, "Lousy graphics." Hannah nodded and turned her attention back to the screen. The movie was beginning. A man was kissing a woman passionately. "I hope he used his mouthwash," Richard whispered loudly. Hannah was glad when the woman behind them told him to shut up, because she didn't have the nerve to ignore him. He quieted down, and they watched the movie. Hannah held her hands in her lap. She could feel Richard's arm resting on the armrest between them, and she got goose bumps. She decided she still liked him, even though he wasn't perfect, even though he talked during the movies. Maybe he was nervous too. He shifted his arm, and for a moment Hannah thought he was going to put it around her, but he stretched and whispered, "I'm going for popcorn. Want some?" Steve got up when he saw Richard leaving, and Hannah turned to Deirdre. "So?" she whispered.

"We have nothing to say to each other," Deirdre whispered back. "He's so quiet he makes me nervous."

"Talk about the weather. Talk about Christmas vacation."

"And say what? Come on over, my mother and father will be beating each other up?"

"Just don't talk about Pete," said Hannah. "That isn't his favorite subject." She heard shushing behind them. "Watch the movie. I hate people like us."

"Yes, ma'am," said Deirdre.

Richard slid back into his seat and handed Hannah a container of popcorn. "You shouldn't eat it," he whispered, "but I'll give you a break because it's the weekend."

He thought she was fat. Hannah clutched the container but didn't eat any popcorn. He hated her body. The evening was ruined. She could barely focus on the film.

Richard leaned over. "Don't you want any?" he whispered.

"You said I shouldn't eat it," she whispered back, wishing she were a skinny rail.

"I was only kidding," he said, and he took a handful of popcorn and pushed some into her mouth. Reprieved, she ate it.

The credits came onto the screen, and everyone stood and put on their coats. "A happy ending," Deirdre said, yawning, and Steve put his hat on her head, pulling it over her eyes. Deirdre yelled and yanked it off, but she was laughing. They followed the crowd down the aisle and out into the street.

Pete was waiting there. He was leaning against his car, arms crossed, a border patrol guard. When he spotted Deirdre, he walked toward her and said, "I turn my back and you start fooling around?" He grabbed her arm and pulled her over to him. "I'm not good enough for you, slut?" he said, and Steve lunged toward him. "Cut it out!" he yelled, and Deirdre pushed herself away from Pete and stood in the middle of the sidewalk crying. It reminded Hannah of Popeye and Brutus yanking Olive Oyl around, except it was her friend Deirdre, and Pete looked like he was ready to kill someone.

Hannah rushed over to Deirdre and put her arm around her, but Pete was pulling at her as Richard tried to hold Steve back. People were watching the scene curiously. Deirdre screamed, "Leave me alone, everybody," and started running down the street.

"I have to go with her," said Hannah to Richard, and he nodded, his arm around Steve. Pete turned to her and pointed his finger accusingly. "You've turned her against me, you bitch," he said, and got into his car.

When Hannah reached Deirdre, she had stopped running. Hannah walked beside her without saying anything. Tears were streaming down Deirdre's face. Hannah fished a tissue out of her pocket and handed it to her.

Deirdre held it to her nose and continued walking. "I don't know where I'm going and what I'm doing," she said in a muffled voice. "I can't go home."

"Come home with me," said Hannah. "You can sleep at my house." Deirdre started sobbing again, and she was walking unevenly, slipping on the ice until she had to hold on to Hannah. "I hate him," she whispered, "and I can't stay away from him."

They reached Hannah's house and went directly upstairs to her room. Deirdre threw herself across the bed, still in her coat. Hannah watched her like she was watching a play on the stage. She was beginning to feel removed from the drama.

She felt like an intruder knocking on her parents' bedroom door. She tapped so softly that she had to take courage and knock harder.

"Mom?" said Hannah, sticking her head around the door. "We're back. Can Deirdre stay over? She's kind of upset. Pete was there." She hated asking her mother for anything, in the rarefied atmosphere of her mother's depression.

Mrs. Gold put down the book she was reading. "Tell her she's welcome to stay over," she said, "but have her call her mother." She pulled the covers around her and picked up her book again.

Hannah stood in the doorway. "Are you okay, Mom?" she asked. "Where's Dad?"

"He went to play cards. I'm fine, honey," said her mother. "It's hard growing up, isn't it?"

The telephone rang, and Hannah ran to answer it. It was Richard.

"Is everything okay?" he asked.

"Fine," said Hannah, enjoying the drama again. "She's sleeping over. I can't stay on too long because she has to call her mother."

"I'll make it quick."

"Don't rush," said Hannah, thankful that he couldn't see her blush.

"It's about the Christmas concert on Tuesday. A couple of us are going, and I wondered if you wanted to meet me there."

"Sure," said Hannah. She threw caution to the wind. "I'd love it. School vacation starts and I can stay out later."

"Good." Richard paused. "I'll drive you home."

Hannah got off the phone and sat down in the bright kitchen. Dirty dishes were in the sink. Not like her mother. Maybe Arizona would help. She could hear water running upstairs. Deirdre, fixing her face perhaps. Hannah straightened her shoulders and readied herself to give her best friend a pep talk. A picture of Bobby flashed across her mind. It had been fun, ice-skating on the river. She shook the picture away. Mr. Kreutzer prowled close by, and she shook him away, too. He had gone to Florida on vacation. Maybe the plane would crash. She tried to concentrate on the feeling of elation. After all, it was almost a date with Richard. Some other time she would ask Deirdre what she should wear to the concert. Not tonight. Tonight she was looking for a happy ending.

Hannah's mother put two dishes of scrambled eggs in front of Deirdre and Hannah.

"Eat up," she said. "You look worn out. Get some protein into you." She sat down and spooned some oat bran cereal into her mouth. "I'd offer you oatmeal," she added, "only I was pretty certain you'd say no."

"I would," said Deirdre, making a face. "Any doughnuts around?" she asked hopefully.

"In this house?" Hannah snorted. "Mom goes by Jane Brody's column in *The New York Times.*"

"Who's Jane Brody?" asked Deirdre, spreading raspberry preserves on a piece of whole wheat toast. "Never mind, I can guess. She's a psychologist or a psychiatrist or something."

Mrs. Gold laughed, sputtering the coffee she was drinking. "What kind of reputation have I gotten myself? She writes a health column." She put down her coffee cup. "But while we're on the subject, Deirdre"—she cleared her throat—"a talk with someone professional wouldn't hurt."

"About what? Nutrition?" said Deirdre, nibbling on her toast.

"No," said Mrs. Gold, glancing at Hannah. "About anything that's bothering you. Mount Hebron Guild, in town . . ."

"Forget it," Deirdre burst out angrily. "I'm not the crazy one. My mother is."

"That may well be," said Mrs. Gold quietly. "But her craziness affects you. Just think about it, will you?"

"Why don't you send Hannah?" said Deirdre bitterly. "She's not the happiest person I know."

Hannah sucked in her breath, kept her mouth shut, tucked away the word *bitch*.

Mrs. Gold smiled gently. "At some point in our lives, maybe we could all use some outside help." She looked at Hannah. "I'm telling Hannah the same thing."

"I can solve my own problems," said Deirdre. She stood up and scraped the uneaten egg off her plate into the garbage can. Turning to Hannah's mother, she said, "A little junk food never hurt anyone," and walked out of the kitchen.

Hannah's mother left for Arizona early on Tuesday morning. Hannah stayed in bed, listening to her mother give last-minute instructions to her father.

"Don't talk to me from the other room," called her father, and Hannah could hear her mother's brisk footsteps on the wooden floor.

"I said I've gotten food in for my mother. . . . She's coming to hear Hannah play on Wednesday and will stay for the week. She'll make chicken soup and chopped liver . . . and you and Hannah won't be so lonely."

"Oh, God, she'll talk us to death," said Mr. Gold. Hannah was surprised. Her father liked her grandmother. He sounded like Hannah when she was in a rotten mood, except her mother would have said, "Watch your tone of voice, young lady."

Hannah heard a scraping noise and strained her ears to hear more clearly.

"I'll get that," said her father. "What have you got in here? It weighs a ton!" Hannah roused herself, threw off the covers, and slipped into a bathrobe. At the doorway she stopped.

"Hannah's going to the school concert with that Richard character," said Mrs. Gold. "I hope she doesn't get hurt. She's so sensitive. This one is her big crush, you know."

"She'll get over it. Plenty of fish in the sea."

They had him breaking up with her before they even went out. Hannah stood there, frozen in place.

"I know his mother, you know. She belonged to the Democratic Club. What a witch! And arrogant!"

"And you figure like mother, like son?"

Her mother's answer was muffled. She heard her father's voice very clearly.

"Maybe absence will make the heart grow fonder."

Her mother's voice rose in a fury. "*Spare me,* Ben! My God, I'm married to a two-year-old."

Her father's voice thundered in her ears. "I want to be treated like a man!"

Mercifully the suitcase was being dragged across the floor again. "Where's that cab?" she heard her mother say.

Hannah ignored her slippers and padded barefoot down the staircase. Her head was reeling. What was happening to her parents? Her life was turning into a soap opera before her very eyes.

The doorbell rang. "Phyllis, your cab," her father called. He turned and saw his daughter at the bottom of the stairs. "Honey, you'll catch cold. Put some slippers on." He turned to his wife. "I'll miss you," he said, putting his arms around her and holding her tightly to him. She stood rigid, but at the end relaxed for a second and hugged him. "Good-bye, darling," she said to Hannah, and she held out her arms. "I'm sorry I'm going to miss your orchestra tomorrow." She planted a kiss on Hannah's forehead. "Enjoy yourself tonight. I'll call you in a day or two." She turned and followed Mr. Gold out the door.

Hannah marveled. She couldn't tell they had been fighting. The specter of it hung in the air. Her father came back inside. "The cat's away," he said, squeezing her arm as he passed. "The mice can play," he called back.

Hannah went into the kitchen and poured some cold cereal into a bowl, topped it with some milk, and threw in a spoon. Her father poured himself some coffee. "Breakfast?" he said. "I'm eating in my room today," she answered. She didn't want to talk to him; she didn't want to look at him. The Kileys were beginning to look good to her. They committed all their nasty acts in front of one another, out in the open. Not in secret, like her family.

19

Hannah got ready for her date with Richard silently, almost efficiently. No phone calls to Deirdre, no conferences with her mother to find out which blouse looked better. Her father had never entered into the situation anyway. He always told her she looked beautiful in whatever she wore. Tonight she certainly wouldn't ask him. He was sitting downstairs drinking coffee and eating bread and cheese. Ordinarily she would tell him that he was eating too much cholesterol, and he'd say, "Your mother told me already." Sometimes she would even make him a salad to go with it. Tonight he would suffer. He could harden his arteries and ruin his lungs smoking his pipe afterward. She wouldn't stop him.

"Hannah?" He was calling her from the bottom of the stairs. "Would you like a lift to the high school? It's below zero out there."

What should she do? If she rode with him, she'd have to talk to him. But she didn't want to arrive with frostbite on her cheeks. "All right," she called as coolly as possible. "Be down in a minute."

She looked at herself in the mirror one more time. The

same green eyes. The same turned-up nose—her *"shiksa"* nose. She wouldn't look at her backside, no, she wouldn't. You look fine, she said to herself. She resolved to believe it, without confirmation from her mother or Deirdre or Richard. Or anyone. She would learn to love herself.

Her father pulled the car out of the driveway in silence and swung into the street. Hannah wondered if he knew that she had heard them talking. He reached over and touched her hair, then returned his hand to the wheel. "Always drive with both hands on the wheel," he once told her when he was giving her a driving lesson. When she confused the brake pedal with the gas pedal and almost drove into a drive-in bank, her father suggested that professional lessons might be a good idea. Hannah was relieved. The car in front of them squealed its brakes and screeched to a stop as the light changed to red. The driver had his arm around the girl next to him, and they turned to kiss each other. Hannah looked out her side window. Her father honked his horn when the light turned green, and the driver stuck his hand out the window and flipped him off.

"Punk," said Hannah's father. "Speaking of punks, how's Deirdre doing?"

Hannah couldn't help smiling. "She's still with Pete, if that's what you mean. It's on and off." She flipped the car visor down and inspected her face in the mirror.

"You look beautiful," said her father. "A knockout." He pulled the car up to the high school and switched off the ignition. "Maybe I should go to the concert. With your mother away my social calendar is pretty empty."

Hannah looked sharply at her father. He was filling his pipe with tobacco. "Thank goodness you waited until I was out of the car," said Hannah. She could feel the anger welling up again. "Why do you want to smoke that thing anyway?" she said. "Are you trying to kill yourself?" She felt her eyes fill up with tears. She saw her father dead, and in a flash she saw her grandfather's laughing face, she heard him calling her Hannahleh. Gone.

"What's the matter, honey?" asked her father. He rested the filled pipe on the dashboard. "What's bothering you?"

"It's you and Mom!" cried Hannah. "I hear you. Screaming at each other." She hid her face in her woolen scarf.

Her father didn't try to look at her. He spoke quietly in the direction of the windshield. "We're having our problems," he said. "I'm sorry you hear us. I hate to hear it myself."

"Are you and Mom going to get a divorce?" Her voice was muffled.

"No!" His voice was close to her ear now. "Your mother and I will work things out." He tugged gently on the end of her scarf. "Now stop smothering yourself and go and have a good time."

Hannah raised her head. "Is my makeup messed up?" she asked.

"You look lovely," said her father. "Did I ever tell you how much you look like Ingrid Bergman when she was young? And Diane Keaton."

Hannah opened the car door. "Diane Keaton? That's a new one!" She laughed and slammed the door shut. Her father turned on the motor, and she knocked on the window. "And stop smoking!" she yelled through the glass. Mr. Gold smiled, and with a wave he drove off.

Hannah fluffed out her hair as she walked up the steps to the school entrance. Where was Richard? Would she have to go into the auditorium alone? She pulled off her gloves. Her hands were perspiring now, and she wiped them on her coat. There was Richard, standing at the entrance. She willed him not to take her hand. Not yet.

They went inside and she watched him pay for two tickets. Her hands were still sweating. She put her gloves back on. Richard handed her a ticket and waved away her proffered wallet. "Thanks," she said. He took her gloved hand and they went into the auditorium.

Steve had saved seats for them. "Hi, Hannah," said a voice, and Pam leaned forward in her seat next to Steve. "Merry Christmas. I mean Happy Hanukkah, right?"

"Right," said Hannah, and she tried not to stare at the sprig of shiny holly pinned at Pam's cleavage. Her heart sank. Did this mean they would all go out together afterward? The lights dimmed and the choir filed onto the stage. The first song was "The Holly and the Ivy." Hannah looked over at Pam. She was imitating a conductor, and her breasts were moving rhythmically under her thin blouse. Hannah forced herself to look away. No more breast envy. She pulled off her gloves and tried to wipe her hands surreptitiously in her lap. Richard took one, and her sweaty hands didn't matter anymore. His hand was cold and clammy.

She enjoyed the concert. They sang only two Hanukkah songs, but the music was beautiful. Hannah's grandmother liked to tell her that she used to sing in a church choir until her father found out and made her quit. Grandma knew all the words to every Christmas song.

At intermission Hannah stood and stretched. Richard

was busy talking to Steve, and Pam leaned across them. "Do you want to go to the ladies' room?" she said to Hannah.

Mary Plunkett was at the bathroom mirror. She gave Hannah a hug. "You look great!" she said, and lowered her voice. "Nice going. Richard's a doll."

"Isn't he?" Hannah gave Mary a pinch on the arm.

"You're a regular Ken and Barbie couple," said Pam, checking to see that her bra straps were hidden. She ran a comb through her hair and pursed her lips at her reflection. "See you back there," she said.

Mary waited for the door to close. "She's just jealous," she said. "The two of you look great together." Mary stepped into a vacant stall and called through to Hannah, "So what do you think of my date?"

Hannah brushed her hair vigorously and said, "I didn't see who you were with! Tell me."

"Only the class clown. Bobby Mack."

Hannah stopped brushing in midair. She heard the toilet flush. Mary emerged and leaned over the sink to wash her hands. "I never knew he was even interested. I mean, out of the blue he asks me to go." Mary held her hands under the hot-air blower. "They should have a sign on this thing: 'Shake excess water off hands, hold under hot air, and wipe on pants.' Who dreams these things up?" Mary wiped her hands on her pants. "I mean, I always thought he had the hots for you. He was always watching you or teasing you."

"Teasing me? More like torturing me." The brush was shaking in her hand, and Hannah threw it in her purse. "Ready?" she said to Mary. They walked back to their seats, and there he was, two rows ahead. How could she have missed him? Hannah was relieved when the choir filed on stage again, but after every song her eyes were drawn to the back of Bobby's head. He never turned around, and she had to force herself not to lean forward to see if he was holding Mary's hand. She hoped it was cold, wet, and clammy.

At the end of the concert the principal lit the candles of a large menorah and plugged in the Christmas tree. As the colored lights flashed on, he wished everyone a happy holiday and a prosperous and education-filled new year.

"He's a riot," said Richard, stretching his arms as he stood up. "What did he give his wife for Christmas, a dictionary?"

Hannah kept her mouth shut. On her father's last birthday her mother had given him a beautifully bound dictionary on a stand. She put on her coat and stuffed the program into her pocket. "My father reads a lot," she finally blurted out. "My parents belong to a reading club."

"Stephen King's okay," said Richard. "I don't know about a reading club."

"Poor Richie reads himself to sleep, don't you, Richie?" Pam said. She gave him a push. "Let's get going. Steve and I crave a pizza."

"Sure," said Richard. He leaned close to Hannah and whispered in her ear, "Big girls like that need sustenance." "Sexist," she whispered back, but she was glad he hadn't said it about her. She would have died on the spot. She shook her head. No, she wouldn't. Banish the thought. She just wasn't ready to have her shaky resolve to love herself tested yet. As they moved to the end of the row Hannah saw that according to her calculations, she was heading straight for Bobby Mack. She looked into his green eyes. His blank green eyes. "Hi," she said in her friendliest tone of voice. He nodded and gently pushed Mary toward the door. Mary turned and winked. "Don't do anything I wouldn't do," she called gaily.

"Speed it up," said Pam. "I need feeding." She linked an arm through Steve's and said, "I'm driving. Little Stevie doesn't have his license yet."

Steve laughed. "That's why I date older women," he said. "That and their voracious appetites." He looked knowingly at Richard, and Hannah wished for a moment that she were home with her father watching *Double Indemnity*. Barbara Stanwyck always knew what to do with her men. She ate them up alive, her father said.

They decided to meet at Joe's Pizza Parlor and headed for their separate cars.

"I didn't know you got your license," Hannah said as Richard unlocked the door.

"I've got my permit," Richard said in a low voice, ushering her into the car.

"You need a licensed driver in the car," protested Hannah, moving to get out of the car.

"A mere technicality," said Richard, pushing her gently back into the car and closing the door. He knocked briskly on the driver's window. She leaned over and unlocked his side of the car.

"You're safe with me," said Richard in a teasing voice. "Driving, that is."

Hannah strapped herself in. She was having a hard time saying no, that was for sure. Her father would be furious if he knew. It was so much easier saying no to a guy you didn't like.

When they arrived, Pam and Steve were already sitting at a table. Pam had sprinkled a pattern of oregano and Parmesan on the placemat and was drawing in it with her fork.

"It's a picture of Stevie!" she said triumphantly. "Is that a Rembrandt or what?"

"More like Picasso's Parmesan period," said Richard, giving the placemat a little shake.

"Or pointillism," said Hannah. She wondered if they knew what she was talking about. "You know, all those little dots that Georges Seurat painted?"

"Georges who?" said Pam. "What's your point?" She looked blankly at Hannah, then burst out laughing. "Get it? What's your *point*?"

"Okay, Joan Rivers, what are we eating?" Richard swatted her with a menu. "What do you feel like, Hannah?"

"We already ordered for you," said Pam. "A mushroom and sausage pizza. You like sausage, don't you, Richie?"

"Is the pope Catholic?" said Richard. "Actually, the pope may be, but Hannah isn't. Can you eat sausage?"

"I'll manage," said Hannah. "My mother won't keep that stuff in the house because of the nitrates. So sometimes my father and I have secret bacon-and-egg binges at the diner."

"Richie can always pick the sausage off for you, like a good rabbi. Can't you, Richie?"

"Right, Pam." Richard concentrated on turning his glass of ice water and the container of sugar into a percussion section.

Pam leaned forward, her eyes wide. "Really, Richard, I thought you liked Catholic girls better." She gestured toward Steve. "Stevie does, don't you? They're hotter!"

Steve looked blank for a moment. "Catholic girls? Ohhhhhh." He licked one finger and made a sizzling noise.

Hannah felt her face redden. It occurred to her that Pam might be jealous. She let a new feeling surge through her, envelope her. She felt it when she played her violin. She felt it when she turned in a particularly good essay. She hardly ever felt it with boys. She wanted to feed the new feeling, nurture it. Never let it go. She was beginning to feel confident.

Richard put his arm around Hannah, and she leaned into it. "Hannah is the exotic type," he said. "We get tired of white bread."

Hannah laughed easily. "What am I, pumpernickel?"

"With raisins," said Richard. "Definitely with raisins."

"How did you know I had freckles on my back?" she said, enjoying herself.

"Hannah is a cinnamon-raisin bagel if ever I saw one," announced Steve. "And Rich is a loaf of Italian bread. A long one."

"And a day old," said Pam. "Hard and crusty." Steve and Richard hooted, and Pam cupped her chin in her hands and said, her voice creamy, "So what am I?"

Steve took out a pair of glasses from his shirt pocket and, expelling a long "hmmmmm," examined her with great seriousness. "A cupcake," he said finally. "No. Two vanilla cupcakes, with cherries on top." Pam squealed with laughter, and Hannah watched the silent exchange of looks again. She couldn't help thinking that a cinnamon-raisin bagel was much nicer. More wholesome, anyway.

The pizza arrived, and Hannah took the slice with the most sausage on it. "Delicious," she said, biting into it with relish.

Richard took Hannah's hand as they left the pizza parlor. They reached their cars and Hannah was thankful that no mention was made of meeting up with Steve and Pam at some other destination. The boys gave each other thumbs up, and Hannah hugged Pam impulsively. They were equals now, and Hannah bore her no malice. Pam kissed Richard soundly on the lips and said, "Merry Christmas, sweetie." She winked at Hannah. "Hope you don't mind. I'm feeling the Christmas spirit."

Hannah was feeling it, too. Her heart was racing as she belted herself in. She no longer worried about Richard's lack of a license. It was the rest of the evening that occupied her thoughts.

A kiss on the cheek startled her.

"Hope she didn't give you too hard a time in there," said Richard. "We went out a few times. Sour grapes or something." He started up the motor and said casually, "How about a midnight drive?"

"Terrific," she said, glancing at her watch. It was eleven o'clock and her father had asked her to be home by twelve. What the heck. "Drive carefully, James," she said in a regal voice.

"Your wish is my command, madam," said Richard, and he pulled out into traffic.

Hannah loved driving at night during Christmastime. The Christmas lights were different at each house. Discreet little white ones on a single tree. A spectacle of light at the next house. A manger, and then a giant candy cane suspended from a roof. A single wreath. They passed them all, and Hannah kept her eyes glued to the window.

"Aren't they great?" she said. "Look at that house with the Santa Claus and his reindeer."

Richard laughed. "What's a nice Jewish girl like you doing looking at the Christmas decorations?"

"I love them," she said. "It's funny. I hate fireworks during the Fourth of July. Everyone goes wild for them. I hate them. But I love Christmas lights."

"That's not hard to figure out," said Richard. "You don't like noise." He turned down a side street.

"I don't think that's it," said Hannah. "Christmas lights are so . . . clean. They're just there to be beautiful. Fireworks are so . . . nebulous."

"Whatever you say," said Richard, laughing again. "You're nuts."

"No, I'm not!" Hannah leaned toward him and pushed gently against his shoulder.

"Why don't you stay right there," he said.

"Because I have to wear my seat belt!" Hannah laughed.

"Give me a break." Richard's voice was hard and sarcastic.

She hesitated but left it on. Her confidence was shaken by his tone of voice. She hadn't pleased him, and he had turned on her. Hannah tried to fill the silence with more conversation.

"We celebrated Christmas once," she said.

"Oh, yeah?" he said. He jammed his hand against the horn and yelled, "Get off the road, asshole!"

Hannah continued. "One Christmas my sister and I begged my parents to hang up stockings. We drove them crazy about it!" She glanced sideways, her hand on her seat belt, ready to unlock it if only his frozen face would melt.

"So what happened?" His face relaxed a little, and he smiled. "Don't keep me in suspense."

"They gave in. They did it. The next morning we woke up and found two little stockings with our names on them, full of presents."

"And you converted and lived happily ever after."

"No, that's the point. The following year, they said they made a mistake. There would be no more stockings. We were Jewish and that wasn't the Jewish way of celebrating."

"Poor baby."

"Oh, we got over it. We had little presents for eight days, we lit the menorah and sang songs. What shook me up wasn't the stocking being taken away. It was that they said they made a mistake. I thought parents never made mistakes."

"You've got to be kidding. My father *is* a mistake."

The houses and Christmas lights were gone now. A frozen lake appeared on her left, and rows of trees and snow-covered picnic tables on her right. Hannah suddenly realized where they were. Echo Lake Park. Ahead she could see a row of dimly lit parked cars. Richard pulled into an open space, and Hannah heard the snow crunch under the tires.

Richard switched on the radio and unhooked his seat belt. "Come on over," he said, and pulled her to him.

"Ouch," said Hannah, "I'm strangling in this seat belt." She unhooked it and slid next to him. She wondered if he could hear her heart hammering under her jacket, and her lips met his lips as they kissed. She pulled away and said, "My lips are chapped," and he pulled her back toward him, saying, "Let me give you some of my Chap Stick." She laughed and kissed him some more, thinking this wasn't so bad and pushing back the thoughts of fireworks and bells and old romantic movies, because this was Richard and she had dreamed of Richard all year. The radio jingled cheerfully away, Stevie Wonder singing an old hit, "My Cherie Amour," and she thought, This could be our song, except they only play it on the radio once a year. And then he put his tongue in her mouth and she no longer heard the music, and he was probing her teeth and her gums and her tongue and it was Mr. Kreutzer all over again. She pushed Richard away and said, "It's getting cold, isn't it?"

Richard smiled and retrieved her, whispering "I'll warm you up" and kissing her some more. She forced herself to think of Richard, and she was glad her braces were gone and all those years of not smiling in photographs were over, and then Mr. Kreutzer was back, wet and sweating. No, he would not ruin it for her, he would not, and she kissed Richard back like they did in the movies, with lots of feeling and passion. Didn't her pizza mouth bother him? Some of the girls carried little mouthwash sprays around with them, especially the smokers, and Hannah wished she had one with her. But Richard kept kissing her and murmuring, "You're so sweet, Hannah," and she guessed he didn't mind at all.

Hannah's feet were getting cold, and she stomped them up and down for a moment, but Richard kept kissing her, his hands in her hair and stroking the back of her neck, and she felt the zipper of her jacket being pulled down. Now his hand was inside her jacket, rubbing on top of her sweater, and she wished that she felt more, a little more. She couldn't fake the Hollywood style anymore, but she tried to kiss him back with interest—maybe it just took time, that was all. She ran her fingers through his hair, but her body stiffened as his hand found the V neck of her sweater and entered stealthily, finding her breast and massaging away. She wasn't afraid, but she couldn't decide whether to push him away or not, because she would have to at some point. But when? Then a blinding light was shining in her eyes, and she gave a cry and pushed away as she caught a glimpse of two eyes and a gigantic flashlight peering in through Richard's window.

Richard pushed back against the seat with a thump and cried "Shit!" as he rolled down the window, and the police officer stuck his head halfway through.

"You folks can just move on now," he said. "The park is closed at sundown, and you two don't seem to be enjoying the scenery." Hannah could hear the sound of motors starting up, and Richard switched on the ignition without a glance at her, and she watched the police officer get into his car and drive away. She was glad she couldn't see Richard's face.

"Let's get out of here," he said, putting the car into reverse. They heard the tires spinning furiously. He gave the car some gas, but it didn't move, despite Richard's pumping and cursing. He shut off the motor and slumped in his seat. "I can't believe this," he said. He sat there for a few seconds, then pulled the keys out of the ignition, still not looking at Hannah. He swung open the car door and unlocked the trunk, removing a shovel, and began digging the snow away from the tires. Hannah got out and stood next to him, feeling helpless. "Can I do anything?" she asked him, but he shook his head and continued digging away at the tires. "Get back in the car," he said tersely. Then they listened again to the spinning and whining of the wheels. Richard groaned, and Hannah had the urge to laugh but stifled it quickly. "Come on," she said, "it's an adventure." Richard turned and looked at her, no sign of loving her sweetness in his eyes. "I have to call my father," he said, crunching off into the snow as he headed for the road. "Are you coming?" he called, and Hannah followed.

She hooked an arm through his, but there was no squeeze in return, no sign that he was glad her hand was there. "My father is going to kill me," he said. They walked silently along the dark road, and when a car passed Hannah said, "We could hitchhike," knowing that this wouldn't please him. Richard looked at her with loathing. "And leave the car here?" he said angrily. "Great idea." They continued walking, and finally they reached a phonebox just outside the park entrance. Richard spoke quickly, and she heard him give directions to the parking area.

They walked back, and this time Hannah did not try to take his arm. He hardly noticed her, and walked with his head hunched into his jacket and his hands deep in his pockets. Only once, when Hannah slipped on a patch of ice, did he lift his head and look vacantly at her, murmuring "careful" and assuming the hunched position again. Hannah could have been walking with a stranger.

They sat in the car, waiting. It was like an icebox, but Hannah didn't dare ask him to turn on the heat. It was her punishment, she assumed, for an evening she had looked forward to that had ended in disaster. She felt sorry for Richard and put a hand on his shoulder. He shifted slightly and turned to her. "Look," he said. "I know I'm acting like a bastard. My father is going to give me hell, and I just want to get it over with. It has nothing to do with you." Hannah nodded and wondered how Richard's father could be any more frightening than the police officer. Her heart started hammering again at the thought of it. And she saw Richard with his hand in her sweater. She squirmed in her seat and tried to push the image from her mind. She concentrated on warming up her hands. She rubbed them together and blew on them, then tried blowing in her gloves and putting them on immediately. Richard sat behind the wheel, his gloveless hands resting on it, frozen in place.

They both sat up straight in their seats when they heard the sound of tires crunching on snow, and Richard moved slowly, opened the door reluctantly. Now that the moment of confrontation was here, he slowed his movements to a snail's pace and turned to look at Hannah. Hannah thought of a blindfolded prisoner facing a firing squad and smiled at him.

Richard's father was smaller than Hannah had imagined—he looked a little like Danny DeVito, a fierce little bulldog. Richard was a good six inches taller, and much better looking. The little man's eyes were narrowed in anger, and he stared at Richard for what seemed like a full minute before he uttered his first and only word of the evening. "Dummy," he said. Then he opened the back door of his car and motioned for Hannah to enter, and when they had locked their seat belts, he drove off. Richard's car, imprisoned in snow, was Hannah's last glimpse of Echo Lake Park.

Hannah breathed a sigh of relief as she let herself into the house. The living room light was on, and it reflected off the metal of the music stand. She switched it off as she went up the stairs, and told herself that she would have to practice in the morning. An interrupted snore came from Jean's old bedroom and she realized that Grandma must have arrived. No wonder she thought she smelled stuffed cabbage when she entered the house. Her father called out, "Is that you, Hannah? Is everything all right?" She called back, "We got caught in the snow, and Richard's father had to come get us." There was a short silence, and she held her breath. Then her father said, "As long as you're home safe." Hannah put on her nightgown and brushed her teeth with the door open and heard her father call, "My own special French toast for breakfast." She smiled and said, "Great, Daddy." Then she rinsed her mouth with water. Her grandmother snored loudly from the other room, and Hannah walked into her room and shut the door.

20

Grandma had gone to countless concerts—anything that featured her grandchildren, she was there. When Jean had sung in a Christmas concert at the Port Authority, Grandma was an hour early, sandwiched in between the bums and the travelers, craning her neck to see her grandchild. When Hannah's orchestra played a concert at a hotel in Atlantic City, Grandma took the train there, despite Grandpa's protests. And no matter how tinny the orchestra, how discordant the playing, she embraced Hannah afterward, her eyes brimming with tears. "So beautiful," she said. "Like angels."

Hannah entered the foyer outside the auditorium, violin in hand, looking for her grandmother and father. There were Grandma's outstretched arms, and she ran into them, embarrassed. Looking around, she saw Bill being embraced by an older woman. She heard the shrill voice of George's mother in the corner: "My son the musician." No one was spared, and she gave herself up to the embrace and kissed her father, too. He looked at Hannah and said, "It was wonderful, sweetheart. How about celebrating at the diner of your choice?" She gave him a smile—they had celebrated with ice cream sundaes for as long as she could remember—but Hannah longed for their own cozy kitchen tonight. She waved to George on the way out and he waved back. Perhaps he had forgiven her. Mrs. Goldberg turned her head sharply away. How could anyone who gave up her son be forgiven?

Bill Tuttle was nowhere to be seen. Perhaps he had disappeared into some diner of his choice with his mother and a loving girlfriend. Hannah realized she didn't care.

When they arrived home, Hannah put a kettle of water on the stove, and Grandma took out a quart of mocha chocolate-chip ice cream and three dishes.

"Your mother would have given me frozen yogurt," said Mr. Gold, eating guiltily from his dish. He glanced over his shoulder. "I feel like a thief. Like she can see what I'm doing all the way from Arizona."

Hannah laughed. "You make her sound like a prison warden," she said.

"She takes good care of you, Ben," Grandma said sharply, rising as the kettle whistled. She immersed a single teabag into a cup of steaming water, dipped it several times, and repeated the process in the next cup. "We all know my daughter is perfect," she said, placing a cup of weak tea in front of Hannah's father.

"Like her mother," said Mr. Gold, smiling. "But, Mom, you could have used three teabags."

"Hush," said Grandma. "I saved you money."

Hannah's father stood and kissed Grandma on top of her wiry-haired head. "Thank you," he said. He turned to Hannah. "Honey, do you mind if I take this delicious cup of tea upstairs?" He eyed the ice cream. "If I stay, I'm liable to have a second helping of cholesterol."

Hannah waved him away, and he leaned over and planted a kiss on her cheek. "I'm so proud of you," he said.

Grandma settled in her chair, blowing on her steaming cup of tea. Then she scooped a helping of ice cream into her dish. "My cholesterol is fine," she announced. "The doctor tells me I'm as healthy as a horse." She mushed up her ice cream like a child. "Grandpa always made fun of me, but I like it soft," she said defiantly. She ate a mouthful. "So why shouldn't I enjoy myself? Speaking of enjoying yourself, how was your date last night?"

Hannah choked on a mouthful of tea. "Don't ask, Grandma." She dabbed her mouth with a napkin. "Let's just say that next year had better be an improvement on this year."

Grandma lifted her teacup and clinked it against Hannah's. "I'll drink to that," she said. "But wasn't this the fellow you carried a torch for all year?"

"Yup. Richard." Hannah scraped the bottom of her bowl with her spoon. "We kind of double-dated, and Pam, the other girl, was a pain in the butt, if you'll excuse my French. She was all over Richard."

"And? Did she like this Richard?"

"Probably. They went out once or twice." Hannah bent down and pulled off her shoes. "My feet are killing me in these heels." She massaged her toes and, not looking at Grandma, said, "We went parking afterward and then we got stuck in the snow, and his father had to come get us, and I'll probably never see him again."

"Maybe it wasn't meant to be," said Grandma. She sniffed. "Parking. Your grandpa didn't own a car when we were courting." She gave a dry laugh. "We did it in the bushes."

"Grandma!"

"What? You think only you children kiss in the bushes?"

"No, but . . ." She tried to picture her grandparents making out in the bushes. Passionately.

"I was smart, though. I used protection."

"Grandma, all we did was kiss . . ."

"Good. Keep it that way." Grandma snorted. "I lied to the doctor and said I was married, and he gave me a diaphragm. You think I wanted to end up like my sister? Married and pregnant before she finished high school?"

"Aunt Esther?"

"Sure. Her second husband was a godsend. Paid all her debts from that lousy gambler of a first husband. She and the children nearly died of starvation." She sighed and took a sip of tea. "Your grandpa was a wonderful provider."

"You had a good marriage, didn't you?"

Hannah's grandmother nodded absent-mindedly. "He was a good man." She snapped to attention. "But he drove me half crazy! He was worried to death whenever your mother left the house, whenever I visited my sisters. You'll get mugged, robbed, killed!" She threw up her hands. "We had our problems. Who doesn't?"

Hannah gathered up the dishes, put them in the dishpan, and added soap and hot water. With her back to Grandma, she said quickly, "I'm worried about Mom and Dad." She immersed her hands in the water and cleaned the same plate again and again.

Grandma said quietly, "She misses her father terribly. It was a shock to her system. A terrible shock. And your father. Well . . . your father misses your mother."

"But she's only been away a few days." Hannah turned and faced her grandmother.

"Not that way." Grandma lowered her voice even more.

"We had our hard times, too. When I had the children and I was helping in the store, besides. The shopping, the cooking, the cleaning. I was too tired at night to do anything. . . ." Her voice trailed off. "Do you know what the doctor told your grandfather when he complained? Take another woman." She sipped her tea and shuddered. "Cold. Go to another woman if your wife won't satisfy you."

"What did you do?"

"What any self-respecting woman would do: I changed doctors." Grandma sighed, her famous world-weary sigh, which Hannah's mother had inherited, which Hannah sometimes found herself copying. "Believe me, they'll work it out. They love each other very much." She pushed herself up from the chair with a groan. "These old bones." She straightened her back. "Still. I did more in bed than keep Grandpa's feet warm."

"Grandma!"

Grandma reached over and took Hannah's hand. "Feel this," she said, holding it against her cheek. "My darling girl. Flesh and blood."

Hannah had trouble falling asleep. She was a little girl again, and beady eyes were peering at her through the bedroom window. A filtering of light from the street reminded her of the police officer's gigantic flashlight. Richard's kissing. Could he tell how inexperienced she was? Oh, God, Mr. Kreutzer. The wetness. She moved restlessly in bed, scrunched her pillow into a ball. Go away, go away. Richard's angry face after the car wouldn't start. She would make it up to him. Hannah rolled onto her back and stared at the ceiling. She raised one arm and held it there, the arm swaying back and forth as if it were someone else's.

The blood rushed away from her hand, a dead hand. Her grandfather joined the haunting. Go away, go away. She would make it up to Richard. Make it up to him? She let her hand drop. She hadn't done anything wrong. It wasn't the kissing, or the concert, or anything she said. Her chest felt heavy, and she turned toward the wall and closed her eyes. Go away, go away. Maybe if she opened up the window a little, for a little air, she could sleep. Maybe if she'd let him touch her, down there, but no, the police officer had stopped any more movement. It dawned on her that she was glad the police officer had arrived. Thank you, thank you.

She had a dream. Grandma was sitting on the bed with Hannah, saying "What should I wear?" again and again. She had on Hannah's best jeans, the stone-washed ones, and the doorbell rang. There was a young man at the door, and he said to Hannah, "I'd like Molly's hand in marriage," and he rushed upstairs and lifted Grandma in his arms. Then his face became old, and his dark hair thinned, and he cried, "I can't carry you anymore," and Grandma said, "Please don't let me go, I have protection," and she lay crying on the bed, but when she turned over, Hannah saw that it was herself.

The ringing of the telephone startled her awake, and Hannah leaped out of bed thinking, Richard? Could it be Richard? The clock said eleven. So late? Grandma was cooking something downstairs, and her father's bed was empty. She picked up the telephone in his bedroom.

"Hello?" she said breathlessly. Grandma was on the other line, calling, "Hello, hello," and Hannah said, "I've got it, Grandma. Who is it?"

"Who do you think it is? It's your oldest and bestest friend, dope. How was it?" said Deirdre.

"Not great," said Hannah. "Pam is now officially re-named the Tramp. Where were you all day yesterday? I needed someone to talk to."

"We were out delivering Christmas presents. My mother would give them out, all sugary and sweet, and then in the car she'd open their presents and complain that she married into a family of cheapskates, and then my father would hit the roof. Fun and games."

"I wish my mother was home." Hannah lay back on the bed—her mother's side. Somehow to lie on her father's side was sacrilegious. "She's back the day after New Year's."

"I'd like to send my mother to Arizona with a one-way ticket."

"Deirdre!" Hannah sat up. "Anyway, we went parking, and a policeman interrupted us in the middle of being felt up. Can you believe it?"

"Tell me it ain't so."

"There's more. The car got stuck in a snowdrift, and his horrible father had to pick us up. He called Richard a dummy and didn't say a word to me. His face said 'You're a slut.' " Hannah took a breath. "And there's more. Mary went to the concert with Bobby. 'Don't do anything I wouldn't do,' she tells me, and I don't even know if I was any good at making out or if I even liked it." She sighed Grandma's world-weary sigh. "Then I had a long talk with my grandmother. She said maybe it wasn't meant to be."

"Your grandmother? Boy, you did need me."

"No, really. She told me all about how she used to make out in the bushes with my grandfather!"

"Weird. It's like thinking about your parents having sex. I can't believe mine do. Maybe they do it with pots and pans, hitting each other over the heads."

"I walked in on mine once, and my father had a fit." Hannah debated telling Deirdre about her parents' . . . what could she call it? Rift. "They aren't getting along too well right now," she said cautiously.

"Mr. and Mrs. Freud? I can't believe it."

Hannah didn't want to hear any more jokes. "They love each other. They'll work it out," she intoned like Grandma.

"So what are you doing for New Year's Eve?" Deirdre asked.

"Nothing. How about you? Pete?" Hannah twisted the telephone wire around her finger.

"We went out the night you and Richard had your dream date." Deirdre hesitated. "He hit me."

"What!" Hannah let the wire drop. "What happened?"

"I showed him a pair of jeans that would look good on him. On another boy." There was a silence. "That was a mistake. He let me have it."

"Oh, Deirdre. Stop seeing him, please." Hannah waited.

"I need help. Maybe your mother is right. Maybe I should go see someone."

"When school starts again, I'll walk you over to the guild. The place my mother told you about. We'll make an appointment."

"Hannah?" Deirdre's voice was faint.

"What?"

"Will you still love me if I'm not crazy?"

Hannah laughed. "You'll just be a smarter kind of crazy."

"You want to spend New Year's Eve together?"

"You'll be the best date I've had in ages. Good-bye."

"Wait a second. I have one more piece of advice."

"What? Hurry up, I want breakfast."

"Maybe it wasn't meant to be."

"Witch! Good-bye again!" said Hannah, and she hung up the phone.

Hannah's mother arrived home looking fresher and happier than she had in a long time. Hannah watched carefully as her mother hugged her father. It looked real—her eyes were closed, and she had a smile on her face. "Hello, slimbo," she said to him.

Her father stepped back and hooked a finger in his pants. "I lost a little weight—pining away for you, I think." His face looked boyish and he was grinning from ear to ear. Hannah hugged her mother. "I didn't pine away, Mom, I got fatter."

Her mother laughed. "That's my Hannah. Still worrying about her weight." She pinched Hannah's cheek gently. "I missed you both."

Grandma moved into the circle. "So I don't count? The woman who gave you life?" She hugged her daughter and grabbed Hannah. "We had a good time. I gave my grandchild an old woman's pearls of wisdom. Even though she wouldn't touch my stuffed cabbage."

"She's too much, Mom. Grandma gave me a sex talk!"

"I left her in charge," said Mrs. Gold, smiling. "Grandma's more experienced than I am."

"Deirdre couldn't believe it."

"Maybe Grandma could set Deirdre straight," said Hannah's mother. "Mom, you missed your calling. You could have been a therapist."

"I am," said Grandma. "I just don't get paid for it."

"How was the concert?"

"Our daughter's a brilliant musician," said Mr. Gold.

"Dad!" Hannah watched her father wrap his arms around her mother again. She savored the moment. They were a family again.

21

The first day back at school Richard ignored her in the hallway. Shunned was a better word. Totally. No nod of the head, no faint hello in answer to her greeting. She had been wiped off the face of the earth.

Hannah turned to Deirdre. "Bad breath?" she whispered. "Body odor?" She tried to hide her embarrassment, but her cheeks were burning, and she opened her locker and stuck her head inside, rifling at the bottom for an imaginary book.

"Not bad breath," said Deirdre. "Bad luck." She pulled on a strand of Hannah's hair. "Maybe he needs a few days to get over it."

Hannah searched Deirdre's face. "You think so?" But her friend's face didn't look hopeful, it looked sorry. Hannah fished out a book and slammed her locker shut. "Happy New Year," she said, and they walked to class.

After school, Hannah waited for Deirdre to fix her makeup. She regarded her face in the mirror and couldn't summon up the energy to put on more lip gloss. It was cold outside, and she would be wearing a hat, so why comb her hair? On the wall beside the mirror someone had Magic

Markered LIFE SUCKS! and Hannah felt like signing her name under it.

Deirdre threw her lipstick and hairbrush into her purse and zipped it shut. "Let's go," she said, flicking back her hair. "Is my eyeliner okay?"

"It's fine," said Hannah, pushing her hair under her hat. "But you'll freeze out there without a hat or gloves."

"I'd rather catch pneumonia than mess my hair. Besides," Deirdre added, "I wouldn't mind missing a few days of school. But with my mother home . . ." Deirdre rolled her eyes. "I can't afford to get sick."

"Things aren't any better?"

Deirdre gathered up her books and pushed open the bathroom door. "Things will get better at home the day I leave it." She half-closed her eyes, smiling, and swung her blond hair back. Hannah was beginning to recognize Deirdre's signals that a flirtation was about to begin. She looked around to see who was coming. Steve was at his locker.

Deirdre knocked on the metal door. "Anybody home?" she purred, leaning against the locker.

Steve turned and tried to hide the surprise on his face. "Hey," he said, "what's up?" He shifted awkwardly in place and gestured toward Hannah. "I hear your friend is into icebergs."

"Snowdrifts," said Hannah, wondering how much Richard had told him. "Has his father forgiven him yet?"

"He may never go parking again," said Steve, grinning widely. "He's grounded for a month, but that's nothing unusual."

"He's been ignoring me," said Hannah, immediately sorry she opened her mouth.

"What can I say?" Steve looked around. "He'll get over it." He craned his neck and shouted, "Mitch! Wait up!" Then, with a muttered good-bye, he was gone.

Hannah and Deirdre exchanged glances. "Let's go catch pneumonia," said Deirdre, and they stepped out into the frigid air.

A line of students was filing onto the local bus, and Hannah and Deirdre ran to catch it. Breathless, they took their seats and settled their books in their laps. Hannah stared at the names scratched into the metal on the seat in front of them. "Nancy and Howie, 1984. What do you think happened to them?" she said.

"Married and miserable."

"Or Nancy could be going to college and Howie could be working in his father's business."

Deirdre looked skeptical. "Anyone who carves his name on the back of a bus seat is married and miserable."

"Such a pessimistic view of life," said Hannah. "Just because we don't have boyfriends . . ." She glanced at Deirdre's face and confirmed the statement by Deirdre's passivity. "And just because we don't know what we want to do with our lives—is that any reason for despair?"

Deirdre pointed to the scratched names. "Look at this one—Popeye and Olive Oyl. There was a match made in heaven. How about I write your name—Hannah and a question mark—then the next time we ride on this bus we'll fill in the blank. Which reminds me. I saw Mary Plunkett today."

"And?" Hannah snapped to attention. "What did she say?"

Deirdre widened her eyes. "Such interest?" she said. "Mary had a fascinating story to tell, I must say."

"It's almost my stop and if you don't tell me, I'll drag you off the bus with me."

Deirdre smiled, the cat that swallowed the canary. "Guess where they went after the concert?"

"I'm afraid to ask."

"Home."

"He took her back to his house? Were his parents there?"

"I mean home. He told her he wasn't feeling well, and she went to her house and he went to his house. She was pissed, I can tell you." Deirdre turned and looked slyly at Hannah. "Are you heartbroken for her?"

"You're a wiseguy, and it's my stop." Hannah reached up and rang the bell. "Good-bye."

"I'm happy to inform you I've found the man of your dreams, and you're going to be inscribed on the back of this seat."

Hannah climbed over Deirdre and held on to the seat's metal arm for balance. "Who?" she said as she moved down the aisle.

"Popeye and Hannah. Olive Oyl is definitely out," called Deirdre.

"Good," Hannah called back, "I'll eat my spinach!" And she stepped off the bus.

After dinner that evening, Hannah washed and her mother dried.

"Still food on this one," said her mother, handing a pot back to Hannah. "Vacation's over, you know. Mr. Kreutzer is back from Florida and you'll start your lessons with him this Saturday."

Hannah scrubbed at the pot furiously, soaped it, and scrubbed some more. "I'm not taking lessons from him anymore." The steel wool had turned an ugly brownish color and the water in the pot was swamp water, dank and dirty.

"Leave that one to soak," said Mrs. Gold, squirting dishwashing liquid into the pot and filling it with hot water. "What do you mean, you're not taking lessons from him anymore?"

Hannah let the hot water run in the glass she was holding. "Just what I said." She stacked the glass precariously on top of the dishes already in the drainer.

"That's going to fall," her mother said sharply, removing the glass. "Are you telling me you're giving up the violin?"

"I never said that." Hannah sprinkled cleanser in the sink and concentrated on scouring the white surface. "I'll look around for another teacher," she said, spraying the sink with water.

"I don't know what I'll say to Mr. Kreutzer. He'll be heartbroken." Mrs. Gold sighed. "He's had you since you were a little girl." She threw the towel onto the counter. "I guess we're done. Just empty the drainer."

Hannah took the drainer and wiped away the pieces of food with a paper towel. Then she ran more hot water into the sink, making sure that every speck of dirt was gone. The sink was spotless. She should only feel so clean.

It was early February when Hannah found a new violin teacher. Orchestra rehearsals had begun again, and Hannah asked a few of the violin players who instructed them. She chose the teacher whose name came up twice, Mrs. Singer, and was glad that she was a woman.

Her father made the telephone call to Mr. Kreutzer. He came back to Hannah with a puzzled look on his face and sat down next to her on the couch.

"Did anything out of the ordinary happen between you and Mr. Kreutzer?"

"Why?" Hannah said quickly. "Did he say something?"

"It's what he didn't say," said her father. He rubbed the fine stubble on his chin. "He didn't even ask why." He hesitated. "Did something happen? Please tell me, Hannah."

Hannah looked at her father, concern in his pale blue eyes, a red ridge across his nose from years of wearing reading glasses, a slight sagging of the chin. So worn, so vulnerable. She felt the need to protect him rise into her chest and throat—she wanted to spit it out, to exorcise it. She wanted to be the child and tell him. His pale blue eyes, his weary commuter eyes, were still looking at her.

"Please trust me," she said, and he looked at her and kissed the palm of her hand. "You're growing up," he said as he walked away.

It was also early February when the notes started. Hannah saw the first one taped on her locker and dangling like a flag, her name scrawled across the folded sheet of paper.

She knew it wasn't Deirdre's handwriting, and besides, Deirdre didn't need to leave notes. She opened it up and read:

> A loaf of bread, a jug of wine,
> Please be my early Valentine.

There was no signature, but there was a P.S. that was barely legible: CHECK OUT THE SNAKE IN THE ART ROOM.

Art period wasn't until the afternoon, and Hannah had to sit through math and a tuna sandwich in the cafeteria before she could solve the mystery.

Except the mystery remained unsolved. She made an attempt to work on her collage, pasting pieces of doily and newspaper on a board, sprinkling areas with glitter and paste, and topping it off with an old earring suspended in a blob of acrylic paint, all the while looking around the art room, examining the walls for a sign of a snake.

It was Deirdre who discovered it first. "Maybe it's not a painting," she whispered. "Maybe it's a sculpture." Sure enough, pushed back on the second shelf behind a roll of construction paper and flanked by a Madonna and Child and a three-headed monster was a green snake with a large mouth and a single silver fang. "Now what?" whispered Hannah, and Deirdre reached into the snake's mouth. Pushed way at the back behind the silver fang was a note folded into a tiny square. She handed it to Hannah, and Hannah unfolded it. Inside was a drawing of a tiny heart with a crack through it. "So much for the mystery being solved," said Hannah, tucking the note inside her purse.

"It's kind of sweet, though," said Deirdre. "Maybe it's Richard, and he's too embarrassed to talk to you in person."

"Forget it," said Hannah. "He walks right past me in the hallway without a word. I'm invisible. Look at him." She gestured with her chin toward Richard, who was sitting at a table on the other side of the room. "Does that look to you like a guy whose heart is broken?"

Deirdre shrugged. "Stranger things have happened." Suddenly she grabbed the snake and shouted "Dummy!" Turning it over, she examined the bottom. "Look for initials," she said. Hannah grabbed the snake back and said, "It's my mystery man," but there was no signature to be found.

Two days later she found another note:

> You're cute, you're great, you're really smart,
> You warm the cockles of my heart.

She showed it to Deirdre, but Deirdre could only make a snide comment about the last line, and Hannah said, "Well, I don't care, I'm writing him a note back."

"We're assuming, of course, that it's a boy."

Hannah gave Deirdre a withering look. She took a felt-tipped pen and wrote as artfully as she could: ROSES ARE RED AND VIOLETS ARE BLUE, IF YOU KNOW ME, DO I KNOW YOU?

She showed it to Deirdre. "What do you think? Will the mystery man reveal himself?"

"It will warm the cockles of his heart," said Deirdre, laughing. "But what if it's Gordon, or that guy with the moles that have hairs growing out of them?"

"Thanks a lot," said Hannah. She folded the note and carefully placed it behind the fang in the back of the snake's mouth. "I guess I'll have to take that chance."

Mrs. Kiley was waiting in her station wagon for Deirdre that afternoon, and Deirdre offered Hannah a ride.

"It's easier with you around," she said, and Hannah wedged herself in next to Deirdre in the front seat.

"So how was school, girls?" said Mrs. Kiley. "Deirdre, your elbow is in my way, for God's sake."

"Not bad," said Hannah, trying to catch her friend's eye.

The car swerved around the corner, and Hannah held

tightly on to the armrest, the weight of Deirdre pushing against her.

"I swear they make these roads narrower," muttered Mrs. Kiley. She leaned forward, her head scrunched down in her jacket, squinting at the street, and Hannah was reminded of a little mole, or was it a weasel? "The stop sign!" cried Deirdre, and the car screeched to a halt as Hannah and Deirdre lurched forward and Mrs. Kiley crunched against the steering wheel. "You scared me to death!" cried Mrs. Kiley. "My God, can't you learn to keep your mouth shut? We could have had an accident!"

"Open the door," said Deirdre, and she was trying to claw her way past Hannah, until Hannah practically fell out of the car and into the street.

"That's it," said Deirdre grimly, and she pushed past Hannah and stepped into the slushy snow and onto the sidewalk. "She's killing me." Hannah followed her and reached out to touch her on the shoulder, but Deirdre shrugged her away. "You just don't know," she said, and she continued walking rapidly.

She slowed a little as they reached town, looking listlessly in a window, kicking at a piece of slush. Hannah trailed her, and the medical building came into view. She stopped at the entranceway. "How about it, Deirdre?" said Hannah, coming up behind her. Deirdre gazed at the sign, then looked at Hannah, and she turned to walk into the building. "It beats suicide," she called back.

Hannah's parents were just coming out the door.

22

They were deep in conversation. They breezed past Hannah, who had recoiled in horror at the two rattlesnakes, disappeared behind the gray protective coloring of the supporting column. She melted into the surroundings, became a rock, a statue. Her parents didn't see her. Or Deirdre, for that matter. Deirdre turned, her mouth open, but she took her friend's cue and waited until Hannah's parents had disappeared from view.

Deirdre found her voice. "What were they doing here?"

Hannah blinked as though the lights were turned on suddenly in a pitch-dark room. "I don't know," she answered. She lied as glibly as they did. What were her parents doing coming out of a building full of shrinks and social workers? They'd fed her a pack of lies about family and marriage and love. And Hannah was the last one to know.

Hannah walked boldly to the reception desk and spoke to the woman behind the typewriter there. "My friend would like an appointment for a consultation. She doesn't have much money." Deirdre looked dumbly at Hannah.

The woman consulted a notebook. "It's a sliding scale fee," she said. "I'm sure something can be worked out. How about next Tuesday, around this time?"

Deirdre nodded. The woman scribbled something onto a card and handed it to her. "You're something," Deirdre said to Hannah, tucking the card into her purse.

"No problem," said Hannah. "I've got to get going now." They hugged good-bye and went in separate directions. Hannah turned into the wind, hatless and gloveless. She walked rapidly, head down, and as she rounded the corner her shoulder hit someone sharply; she felt the thud. "Watch where you're going, jerk" was hurled after her, but she kept going, her mind a jumble. They were getting a divorce, she knew it, she felt it in her bones, and one of them would move away, and that would be it, no more tea in the yellow kitchen, just strangeness, just visits. She reached the bench where she had met Bobby a few months ago, and it seemed forever, the ice-skating on the pond, and now she had no one, not Bobby, not Richard, not her parents either, because everything was covered up, it was the Watergate-Gold scandal, and the divorce would erupt on the family from nowhere, except nowhere was a web of deceit and lies and fakery, because they couldn't have ever been happy, could they?

Hannah could see the bright light in the kitchen through the side door. She went in the front door, up the stairs to her room, except there was no real protection here, the rattlesnakes could sniff her out and find her. She heard her mother at the foot of the stairs. "Is that you, Hannah?" She didn't answer.

Her mother proceeded up the stairs. "Hannah?" She

knocked gently at the door to Hannah's bedroom, then pushed it open. "What are you doing sitting here in the dark? In your jacket?"

"I saw you," said Hannah, her voice breaking. "I saw you there."

"Where?" Her mother's voice was bewildered, instantly aware that a volcano was sitting on the raspberry-colored bedspread. "What's the matter, Hannah?"

"I was with Deirdre at the guild, and I saw you!" Hannah rose, her voice harsh and low. "Deirdre's going for some help, just like you told her to. What did you tell me?" Her voice got louder. "What did you tell me? You're going to get a divorce, and you don't even tell your own daughter!" She pushed past her mother out the door, pounding down the stairs. There was nowhere to go except out the front door again, with her father rushing noisily in from the kitchen. "Screw you!" she shouted as she pushed through the door into the frigid air.

The streets were empty. It was suppertime, the commuters were all home with their families, lights were blazing in every kitchen, and Hannah was walking again, her ears freezing, the breath freezing in her nostrils, her feet blocks of ice. The pond at the old mill was frozen solid, empty of children, and she stood watching it, the only fool in the whole world outside in the freezing cold.

A car pulled alongside her, cruising, and she started walking again and tried to ignore her mother's voice calling, "Hannah, please get into the car." The car stopped and she heard the door swing open and her mother called again, "Hannah, we have to talk." Her mother was walking alongside her now, and Hannah turned abruptly and got into the back seat of the car, anything to avoid her mother's persistent presence, a dog yapping at her heels. But her mother got into the back seat, too, and trapped her in the corner, putting her arms around Hannah until she felt rigid like a board.

"We love you," said her mother, "and we love each other, and that's why we were there—to get help—and I'm sorry we didn't tell you." She kept her arms around Hannah, and her breath was so familiar, and Hannah started to cry, saying, "You lied to me," not knowing what she meant, but she continued sobbing and she said, "Mr. Kreutzer put his tongue in my mouth," in between sobs, and Hannah's mother had such a look on her face that Hannah started laughing and hiccuping, and she ended by saying, "I'm sorry I said screw you," and that started her mother laughing, with her father shaking his head in the front seat, the chauffeur of two lunatics.

23

*D*eirdre stuck her finger into the air and made an announcement. "My shrink says I was addicted to Pete because I'm only used to men who treat women badly." She took a wad of gum out of her mouth and unwrapped another piece. She popped the new piece into her mouth and said between chews, "When I feel better about myself, I'll choose nicer boys." Deirdre looked puzzled. "Who's nicer, Steve or that new guy, Craig the hunk?"

"I don't know, but you're addicted to gum, too, because that's the fourth piece you've put in your mouth." Hannah held out her hand. "And I deserve the last piece, because I'm your friend who treats you very nicely."

Deirdre flipped her a piece of gum. "It beats smoking," she said, "and, besides, I have another pack."

"Good. Save it for later, because Mrs. Braddock will call us cows and throw us out of the art room." Hannah slipped the stick of gum into her pocket and sat down at her usual table. They were studying abstract expressionism, and Hannah dripped some paint on a board. "If it's so nice getting all that feeling and expression out, how come I read somewhere that Jackson Pollock killed himself?"

"He had a bad day," said Deirdre, and she swirled some red paint on her board. "He should have gone to a shrink," she added. Deirdre poured a capful of magenta paint on top of her red swirl and lifted the board. "I mean it. No jokes." She watched the paint drip down and headed the drip in another direction by shifting the board. "I think it's really helping. I don't cry in the shower anymore."

Hannah smiled. "I've done some crying in the shower. I like that magenta. Give me some, will you?" She dripped some on her board and scraped into it with the wooden tip of her paintbrush. She scratched a sun into the magenta and suddenly threw down her brush. "The snake!" she whispered. "I forgot about it!"

Hannah searched through a new crop of ceramics and found the snake. She pulled out the usual wad of paper. "Here goes," she said. She read through the note silently and handed it to Deirdre. "Read it."

Deirdre read it out loud:

> The grapes and the figs and the raisins I ate
> Did not fill me up 'cause I'd rather a date.
> (Get the pun?)
>
> R.M.

"R.M.? I told you," Deirdre said excitedly. "Richard still likes you."

"He sure has a funny way of showing it." Hannah lifted up her board and tilted it "Don't mind me, I'm copying you," she said. "So what do I do now?"

"You add some blue," said Deirdre.

"I mean with the note!" Hannah laid down her board and looked over at Richard's table. He was deep in conversation with Steve, and the sight of him didn't send the usual chills up and down her spine. Not like it used to. She turned to Deirdre, surprised. "I don't think I care," she said. "If it's him, I mean."

"You'll break his heart," said Deirdre, and she took her finger, drew a heart, and painted a black crack through it. "Poor Richard."

Hannah sat next to her mother on the couch. She arranged a few cushions strategically behind her and handed her mother the piece of paper. "What do you think of this note?" She reread it over her mother's shoulder.

"A little old-fashioned, but cute," said her mother, handing it back. "Who is R.M.?"

"That's what I'd like to know." Hannah picked up the book her mother was reading and read the flap. *The Good Mother*. How is it? Getting any pointers?"

"Funny girl. The protagonist feels a lot of the feelings that I felt for you when you were little. A mixture of joy and hardship."

"I thought it was supposed to get easier!"

Hannah's mother crossed her eyes and lolled her head. "Does it look like it gets easier?"

"You and Dad are getting along better, aren't you?"

"We're working things out. At least I hope we are."

Hannah looked alarmed. "What do you mean by that?"

"This is the real world, honey. There are just no guarantees." She smiled. "Your father still leaves the cap off the toothpaste."

"You make it sound so hard."

"Hey." Hannah's mother leaned over and took Hannah's

hand, running a finger lightly along her arm. "Do you know what the therapist says?"

"I'm afraid to hear."

"There's no free lunch." Her mother continued tracing a pattern on Hannah's wrist and palm. "But you know what?"

"What?" said Hannah glumly.

"I love to eat." She let go of Hannah's hand. "And I have news for you."

"What!" said Hannah, beginning to smile.

"You have a strong love line."

"I didn't know you read palms."

"I do, I do! Grandma taught me. And you know how smart Grandma is. She loves you, Dad and I are crazy about you . . . and this R.M. character is the first of many." She pointed to the note. "You're sure it's not from Richard? Maybe he's had second thoughts."

Hannah snorted. "He still cuts me dead. And he isn't the old-fashioned type."

"So what about that boy you went ice-skating with? Does his name begin with an *R*?"

"No. His name is Bobby." Hannah sat very still. She felt like the dawn was breaking inside her head. Bobby. Of course. Robert Mack. She grabbed the note and looked at it again. "What do you know. You could be right," she said softly. She started to laugh. He had to sign it Robert Mack! It was too gross to sign it the other way.

"Like I told you!" said her mother.

"What?" said Hannah, smiling widely.

"You have a very strong love line." Mrs. Gold looked mischievous. "I have one more question for you."

"I'm waiting," said Hannah, looking at the crinkles in the corners of her mother's eyes.

"Is he Jewish?"

Hannah spotted Bobby weaving his way up the hall. She turned her head away and rummaged through the locker for her math book. Her heart was beating wildly. She gazed at the book and turned the pages as if it were the most fascinating book in the world. Come over, she willed him. Don't come over.

She felt a touch on her shoulder.

"Hi, Hannah." Bobby stood there, green eyes and a silly grin. "How's life?"

Hannah dropped to her knees and shuffled the books in her locker. "Life's good," she said. "How are you, Bobby?" She turned slightly and fastened her eyes on a pair of battered sneakers.

Bobby took a scuffed sneaker and tapped her on the foot with it. "Call me Bob. It makes me sound more mature."

Hannah raised her head sharply. "Still joking?" she said.

He held out his hand to Hannah. "You have to stand up when I'm being serious," he said as he pulled Hannah to her feet. Suddenly he twirled an imaginary mustache and flicked ash off an imaginary cigar. "What did one strawberry say to another?"

"I don't know, what?" said Hannah, trying hard to keep from smiling.

"If you weren't so fresh, we wouldn't be in this jam." Bobby did a little dance around Hannah.

Hannah gathered up her courage. Her heart was still beating furiously. "Did you write me those notes?" she blurted out.

Bobby stopped dancing. "Yes," he said simply.

"I don't want any more," said Hannah quickly, and she thought he suddenly looked afraid. She rushed on. "I mean, I don't want any more figs or grapes or whatever you wrote."

He looked blankly at her.

"No figs or grapes," she said loudly, aware that the girl at the next locker must think she was crazy.

"Oh!" Bobby started to smile, a grin that extended from one ear to the other, a grin that brought out twin dimples she'd never seen before. "Oh," he repeated, putting his hand in his pocket. He took Hannah's hand and placed a folded piece of paper in it. "Just one more," he said. "I've been carrying this around with me for weeks."

Hannah opened the note. It was a drawing of a single heart, smack in the middle of the paper, with a dab of red paint in the center.

"There's no crack in this heart," she said softly. "How come?"

"I was just hoping," said Bobby. "Was it a mistake?"

"No," said Hannah. She looked closely at his face, at his green eyes and his dark eyebrows, at his straight nose and the little bits of stubble on his chin. "What do we do now?" she said, her face reddening.

Bobby leaned over and, placing his hands on her shoulders, kissed her gently on the lips. Her heart was beating rapidly, faster than an allegro, more like the molto agitato that her new teacher shouted at her when she wanted her to play furiously. It wasn't beating audition fast or exam fast. More like happy fast.

"When did you first know?" said Hannah. "I mean, that you really liked me? I could never tell, you know."

He turned his green eyes toward her and she knew what they meant by a twinkle. "You'll laugh."

"No, I won't," she said, and she took his hand. "Tell me."

"When you played the violin in Mr. Mandel's class. That did it for me."

"You're kidding. And I chose Richard to teach! And I get a double chin when I play!"

Bobby shrugged. "You knocked me out," he said. "Double chin and all."

They walked down the hall together, and Hannah kept her hand in his. It felt strange, like some kind of declaration, but it felt right. She didn't have to hide any side of herself with Bobby. He was sweet and funny and she liked him. Oh, maybe he made too many jokes. Nobody was perfect. She could put up with that. Anyway, growing up was hard enough, and she could use a laugh, once in a while.